Barley and Rye
The Adventure of Lost Castle

SEASON ONE
THE REALM WHERE FAERIE TALES DWELL
STORYVERSE™

REBECCA J. CARLSON

Barley and Rye: The Adventure of Lost Castle, Season One (A The Realm Where Faerie Tales Dwell Series)
By Rebecca J. Carlson
Print Edition Copyright © 2019 by Fiction Vortex. All rights reserved.

This novel is a work of fiction. Names, descriptions, entities, and incidents included in the story are products of the author's imagination. Any resemblance to actual persons, events, and entities is entirely coincidental.

ISBN: 978-1-947655-48-5
Published by Fiction Vortex, Inc. (FV Press)
Nampa, ID 83651
http://www.fictionvortex.com

Cover by Niels Christensen
Illustrations by Rachelle Hoffman

Published in the United States of America

For Daniel, who asked for an adventure with a magic sword.

The Land
Far Away

Lost Forest

Rose Grove Kingdom

Red
Mountains

Troll Hollow

Frog
Pond

Wizard's
Keep

Wi
To

The
Land
Where
Faerie
Tales
Dwell

The Fields
of Sorrow

Knight's Peak

Seaside Kingdom

Wistful Valle

Gloridian

Sw
Tr

Isle
of
Magic

Flying
Island

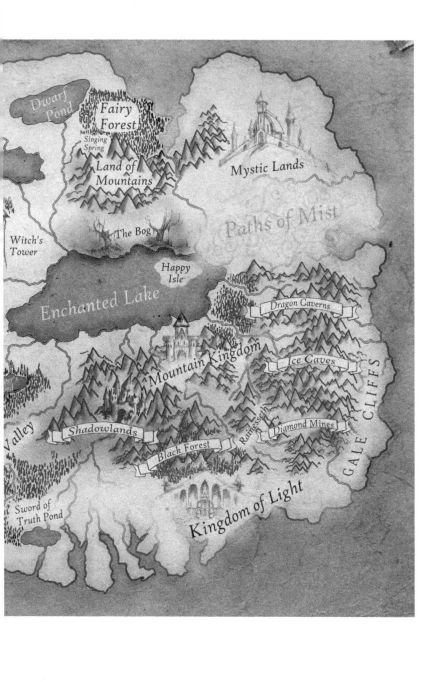

NOTE TO THE READER

Barley and Rye is a series from within the *The Realm Where Faerie Tales Dwell* StoryVerse™ of the Fiction Vortex™ (http://www.fictionvortex.com). You may have gathered that this project involves a growing handful of uncouth authors bent on creating a ruckus amongst the publishing establishment. Shame on us. But kudos to you for boldly stepping into the Vortex.

The Realm Where Faerie Tales Dwell is a StoryVerse™. That means many different authors are creating many different series within a shared story world. You may choose to follow any or all of the series within a StoryVerse. Each series is designed to be enjoyable independently of the others. Of course, the series will enhance each other and shed light on the story world as a whole.

Barley and Rye: The Adventure of Lost Castle is a season's worth of episodic stories in the *Barley and Rye* series. These episodes each tell a story.

No one knows exactly how long each series will end up or how long a StoryVerse will remain open (actively publishing regular content). But we promise that once we start a StoryVerse, we'll end it eventually. No leaving everyone hanging like a certain Fox Studio (cough, *Firefly*, cough, cough).

I suspect that *The Realm Where Faerie Tales Dwell* will easily require a couple years' worth of continual episodes to draw to its climactic closure. But if it balloons in popularity and scope, who knows where it will go before it's all over. This is, after all, a live process depending in no small part on your participation.

ADDITIONAL FAERIE TALES SERIES:

- ❖ Pieces in the Cinders by Emilee King
- ❖ Rose Red by Jessica Parker
- ❖ The Dragon's Maid by Alison Miller Woods
- ❖ Bean Finds a Pet by Alison Palmer
- ❖ Becoming Cinderella by Lecia Crider

For now, enjoy *Barley and Rye: The Adventure of Lost Castle*.

EPISODE ONE: TWO BROTHERS

ONE

Long shadows reached across the lane as Barley and his
brother Rye walked home from helping their father with the
plowing. Father had sent them on ahead while he finished
up the last row. Early summer leaves grew thick in the
hedges all around them, and insects buzzed in the golden,
late afternoon light.

Though they were brothers, the two were as different as
night and day. Barley, the younger one, had golden hair and
a cheerful, round face, while Rye's hair was dark and his face
was thin and clever.

A rustle in the branches of a nearby bush made Barley
pause.

"It's a brigand!" Rye said in a sharp whisper that made
Barley's heart jump. "Quick, Barley! Run for the house. Run
and don't look back! I'm right behind you."

Barley dashed down the road. The Brigands of Lost
Castle were the most feared robbers in the Land Far Away.
They ruled everything on the far side of the river and often
came to Humble Village to snatch away stray sheep and
cows, and even the occasional unwary child.

When Barley ran in through the cottage door, Mother
asked, "Barley, why such a hurry, and where is your brother
Rye?"

"Rye saw a brigand in the road!" Barley checked over his shoulder for Rye. He was nowhere to be seen.

Barley's mother grabbed her biggest frying pan and charged out of the house. Barley followed close behind.

"Where?" Mother asked as they ran.

"Down there," Barley said. Ahead of them the road was empty except for the sunlight and shadows. No Rye in sight. The brigand had taken him!

As they passed the place where Rye first warned Barley to run, a loud crash came from inside the hedge.

Mother held her frying pan high over her head. "Who's there? Show yourself!"

Rye tumbled out of the hedge and into the dusty road. He rolled on the ground, shaking with giggles. "Boo!" He said between gulps of air. "I'm a brigand. Better run!"

Barley felt his face turn as hot as a steaming bowl of porridge. There hadn't been a brigand at all! Rye had only been playing a trick on him.

"Rye! You scared us both to death. I wish the brigands had taken you! It would serve you right!" Mother said.

"What's happened?" Father asked as he came along the lane with their horse, Old Lumpy, on a lead rope.

"Rye said he saw a brigand," Barley said.

"Barley came a-running all the way to the house and said there were brigands in the lane, so I fetched myself out here to give them a good sending-off, but all I could find was this little imp." Mother pointed her frying pan at Rye.

"It's no matter for joking, Rye," Father said. He reached his hand out and helped Rye get up.

"Yes, Father," Rye said, all the laughter gone out of him. In Rye's face, Barley saw the sad memory of all their friends who had been stolen away.

"Tell your brother you're sorry for playing such a trick on him," Mother said. "And tell me you're sorry for scaring me half to death."

"I am sorry," Rye said.

"I know you don't mean any harm," Mother said. She took her two boys into her arms. "You never do. But Rye, you've got to think about how your tricks make folks feel. What if you really had been taken by the brigands?"

"There'd be no one to torment Barley anymore," Father said with a wink.

Two

The next morning, Mother sent Barley and Rye to the river to pick blackberries.

"Stay on our side of the river," she warned. "I don't want the Lord of Lost Castle to catch you and make you his slaves."

"Don't worry, Mother," Rye said.

"We're too quick to be caught," Barley added.

"Like the time you were too quick to be caught putting Old Annie's best Sunday bonnet on Soldier Jack's cow?"

Barley and Rye didn't answer. They both stared upward as if they found something very interesting about the cottage rafters.

Mother laughed. "Off you go. Keep each other out of trouble."

Barley and Rye took their berry buckets and walked down the road to the river. On the way, Rye stopped to turn the head on Goody Butter's scarecrow so its button eyes stared at her cottage door instead of out into the road.

"Should we knock and hide and see if she notices?" Barley whispered. He loved Rye's pranks even if the other villagers didn't always care for them.

Rye shook his head. "No, then she'll know someone did it. If we leave quietly, she might think the scarecrow did it himself."

Trying not to giggle, the boys tiptoed past the Butter's farm and ran the rest of the way to the river.

When they reached the river, they found that all the berry bushes on their side had already been picked over. They walked from the bridge all the way to the bend and didn't see a single ripe berry.

"Of course all the good berries would be on the other side," Rye said. He banged his empty bucket against his knee.

Barley and Rye stood beside the water for a while and watched as it slurped around the rocks. On the far bank, birds pecked at the fat, juicy berries.

"I don't see anyone," Barley said.

"Right, so long as we're quick," Rye said.

The boys balanced across the steppingstones in the shallow river. Once they reached the other side, they walked along the muddy bank, gathering berries. Soon their buckets were almost full.

"Let's go back," Rye said. They had been on the wrong side of the river long enough.

Barley didn't listen. "There's another good patch up ahead. Come on."

"Barley! Wait!" Rye ran after his brother.

As Barley reached for a berry, he heard hoofbeats. Horses! Coming their way, fast.

"Quick, hide in here!" Rye pushed aside the thorny blackberry branches so Barley could climb underneath. Barley scrambled in, then turned to help Rye.

Before Rye could follow Barley, the horses appeared around the riverbend. A man's voice shouted, "Who's there? Is someone stealing berries from the Lord of Lost Castle?"

Rye gave Barley a fierce stare, a finger to his lips. Then he stood up with his bucket behind his back. Three men reined their horses to a stop in front of him. Hidden from view, Barley watched with wide eyes.

"You're under arrest!" one of the men snarled through teeth as crooked as old fence posts.

"For trespassing and stealing," added another, shaking a grimy finger at Rye.

"That's a lifetime of slavery for you, boy." The third one jumped off his horse and caught Rye by the arm. The bucket of berries spilled on the ground.

A single berry rolled beneath the brambles and up against Barley's boot. Too afraid to move, Barley watched as the men tied Rye's hands and feet and put him on one of the horses. They all rode away.

THREE

Barley sat frozen in place under the blackberry bush until
long after the men had gone. The brigands of Lost Castle had
taken Rye away. None of the children from Humble Village
who had been taken to Lost Castle had ever come back. No
one who had gone looking for Lost Castle had ever been able
to find it. Barley knew that no one from the village, not even
his parents, would be able to bring Rye home.

At last, Barley crawled out from under the bush. The
thorns scraped his hands and tugged at his clothes. Part of
him wanted to run home where he'd be safe, but how could
he go home without Rye? It was his fault that Rye had come
across the river. Barley had suggested it first, Barley hadn't
gone back when Rye had asked him to, and now Rye was
gone forever.

Wiping tears from his face with his sleeve, Barley
stooped down to pick up Rye's bucket and noticed
something on the ground. Hoofprints. The hoofprints of the
horses that had taken Rye. They turned away from the
riverbank and took a path through the tall grass.

The horses would be going to Lost Castle. If Barley
followed the hoofprints, he could find the castle, and Rye
too. Then, when he knew where the castle was, he could run
back to the village and get help.

Barley made up his mind. He looked over the river in the direction of home.

"Goodbye Mother, goodbye Father," he whispered, trying to be brave. "Don't worry about me. I'm going to find Rye. I'll be home by supper."

With his bucket of berries hugged tightly to his chest, Barley followed the hoofprints.

FOUR

As Barley walked, the ground became muddier and muddier, the hoofprints sank deeper and deeper, and the grass grew taller and taller. Before long, Barley came to a place where the hoofprints vanished under a layer of gray-black water. No more trail to follow. The pale-yellow grass stood taller than Barley's head. All he could see was a little piece of sky above him. All he could smell was the sour stink of rotting bog. All he could hear was a chorus of ravens cawing. The horse's trail had led him into the middle of Grayfallow Swamp.

If he went any farther, he might not be able to find his way back to the river.

Two ravens flew overhead, and then three more. They all seemed to be going somewhere. Curious, Barley pushed his way through the tall grass to follow them.

The ravens gathered around a small pool. In the pool lay a baby deer that was half sunk in the water. Barley thought it must have gotten stuck in the mud and starved to death. The hungry ravens watched the baby deer and jabbered to each other. One swooped down and landed on its back.

The deer twitched. It was alive!

"Get off!" Barley shouted. The ravens glared at him with angry, black eyes. "Leave it alone!" Barley picked up a handful of mud and threw it at the ravens. They flapped away, cawing and croaking.

After he had driven the ravens away, Barley could not decide what to do next. He wanted to help the deer, but he was afraid he would sink in the mud if he went too close. Besides, he needed to help his brother. He didn't have time to stop.

But if he went away, the baby deer would die.

Barley took a step toward the deer. His foot sank deep in the mud. He gasped and tried to step back, but his shoe was stuck tight. He tugged and tugged until he fell backward onto the wet ground, his shoe stuck in the mud and only his patched sock on his foot.

He wasn't going to solve this by just rushing in. He needed to stop and think this through. Thinking up plans was usually Rye's job, but Rye wasn't here.

Barley worked his shoe out of the mud, put it back on, and then sat for a while and thought. Finally, he had an idea. He pulled up clumps of the tall grass and laid the grass on the pond until he had made a big pile. When he put his foot on the pile of grass, the grass sunk below the water, but it didn't sink below the mud. Carefully, Barley stepped onto the pile of grass, then walked across it until he reached the baby deer. He knelt down beside it and gently lifted it free. Its thin legs were covered in black goo.

Barley carried the baby deer to the side of the pond. He gave it some clean water from his waterskin and fed it some blackberries from his bucket. While the deer ate, Barley used some grass to rub the mud from its legs and stomach.

The little deer stood up. It licked its legs, took one wobbly step, then dashed off into the tall grass.

"Don't get stuck again!" Barley called after it.

The deer came skipping back. It looked at Barley with big, dark eyes, then turned and waited as if it expected Barley to follow him.

"Why should I follow you?" Barley asked. "You got stuck once. You'll probably get stuck again. You'll get us both stuck."

The deer flicked its ears and waited. Then it turned and began to walk away.

Barley followed.

FIVE

At that same moment, Rye got his first look at Lost Castle.

It wasn't a very good look, what with him being draped over the back of a horse, face down. Still, he could tell Lost Castle must have been lost for a very long time to get in such a terrible state. Black ivy crawled over the cracked walls. Broken windows stared out of crumbling towers. Thick, green sludge filled the stinking moat. Rye wished he could cover his nose as they rode across the drawbridge, but his hands were tied behind his back.

At least Barley should be home safe by now. Rye was glad he'd thought of having Barley hide in the blackberry bush. It had fooled the brigands. Maybe he could fool them again and find some way to escape.

The horses rode in under a rusty iron gate that clanged down behind them.

"We've caught another one!"

"Hooray!"

Shouts and laughter filled the courtyard. Many hands grabbed Rye, dragged him off the horse, and set him roughly on his feet.

"Maybe this one knows how to cook," one of the brigands said. Rye wondered if they had all disguised themselves by smearing dirt and soot on their faces, or if they just never bothered to wash.

"Do you know how to cook?" asked a brigand with a wart on his eyebrow.

"I know how to make porridge," Rye said.

The brigands all groaned.

"That's all you runts from Humble Village ever know how to make."

"But...don't you know how to cook for yourselves?" Rye asked.

"Too much work," said a brigand with a broken feather in his hat. "That's why we have you runty ones to do it."

Behind the group of men who had gathered around him, Rye caught sight of a few thin, ragged children poking their heads out of a doorway. He barely recognized Tom Cobbler, the one who had gone missing on a foggy day last winter, and Tildy and Jep Weaver, who had chased after a runaway goat and never come back, and Janet Grover who used to like to wander over the river to pick wildflowers. They stared with sad, empty eyes, so different now from when they all used to play together in the village.

Rye definitely had to come up with a plan. They would all escape. He'd make sure of it.

One of the brigands untied Rye and shoved him toward the doorway. "There you go. Get to work. The others will show you what to do."

Six

Barley had a hard time keeping up with the deer as it hopped over pools and slipped between the tall grass. He was glad when the deer finally led him out into the open at the edge of the swamp.

A steep hillside of sharp rocks rose up in front of them. On the ridge above the rocks stood a forest. Barley knew that Lost Castle must be somewhere in that forest. He had made it through the swamp. Now all he had to do was find the castle.

The baby deer hopped onto the rocks. Its little hooves clattered as it climbed. Barley laughed and climbed up after it. The sharp points of the rocks hurt his hands and poked his feet through his shoes. "I wish I had hard hooves like you," he said to the deer.

The sun was about halfway down the sky when they reached the trees. Exhausted from the climb, Barley sat down at the top of the rocks and looked out over the valley. He could see Grayfallow Swamp below them. On the far side of the swamp, the White River wound past his village. Humble Village looked very small and far away. Even if he started home now, it would be past dark before he got there.

But he wasn't going home now. He couldn't. Not without finding Rye.

Seven

The baby deer nibbled the green grass at the edge of the forest while Barley ate the last of his berries for supper. Suddenly the baby deer raised its head and stared into the trees. It twitched an ear and sniffed the air, then sprang away into the woods.

"Wait!" Barley scrambled to his feet and ran after it. He stopped when he saw a doe standing in the trees ahead.

The baby deer skipped up to the doe. She bent down and licked the baby deer's nose. Barley smiled. "You're home now," he said.

Both deer froze and stared at him, their ears up. Then the mother deer slowly stepped toward Barley. Her hooves made soft sounds in the damp, dead leaves. Amazed, Barley held his breath. All of the other deer he'd seen had run away if he'd tried to get close.

When she was almost close enough for Barley to touch, she stopped and lowered her head. "Thank you for saving my child."

"You're welcome," Barley whispered, surprised to hear the deer speak. He'd heard stories that some of the animals in this forest could talk, but he'd never been sure if he believed them.

"Is there anything I can do for you in return?" the doe asked.

"Do you know the way to Lost Castle?" Barley asked.

"No," the mother deer said.

Barley lowered his head. He couldn't think of anything he wanted more than to save his brother.

"But," the mother deer said, "I will take you to someone who does."

END of Episode One

Episode Two: The Magic Sword

ONE

Barley followed the doe and its fawn through the forest. The woods grew darker. Barley tried not to be afraid.

Then, in the distance, he saw a light ahead.

"There is the place," the doe said. "I will leave you here. Follow the light until you reach the gate, then knock three times."

"Thank you," said Barley.

The doe turned and walked away with her fawn. It was too dark to see them, but Barley could hear their small hooves rustling the leaves. He waited until he couldn't hear them anymore.

Barley felt very alone, even more alone than when Rye had been taken by the brigands. The only thing to guide him was that tiny light in the distance.

Barley fumbled through the trees, his eyes on the light ahead, until he reached a crooked fence with a lantern hanging by the gate. A sagging hut slouched in the yard. Barley knocked on the gate three times.

An old woman came to the door of the hut. Barley's heart thumped hard at the sight of her. She looked like an evil witch out of the stories, dressed all in black with tangled gray hair, a long nose, and shriveled hands. Her spindly limbs stuck out from her round body like the legs of a fat spider.

The old woman's eyes bulged when she saw Barley. Then her face cracked into a grin that showed off three crooked teeth.

Barley took a step back. This had to be a mistake. The deer had brought him to the wrong place. He thought about running, but where would he go, in the woods, in the dark?

"What have we here?" the old woman croaked with glee.

Barley was too terrified to speak.

"How did you find me?" the old woman asked. She squinted one eye shut.

Barley glanced over his shoulder into the dark woods behind him.

"Well, tell me! Speak up!"

Barley swallowed hard. His words came out in a squeak. "The doe showed me the way."

"Oh? And why did she do that?" the old woman asked.

"I found her fawn stuck in the swamp, and I helped it get out so it could go back to the forest."

"Aha! What an unselfish thing to do." The old woman rubbed her hands together. "And what brings you into the forest, young man?"

Barley stood up tall. "I want to find Lost Castle. My brother was taken there." He tried hard not to let his voice shake. "Can you tell me where it is?"

The old woman clapped her hands together. "Yes, yes, of course I can. Please come in. I can tell you the way to Lost Castle, most certainly I can!"

Barley didn't move.

"Come in! What are you waiting for? I don't eat children, you know." The old woman cackled. Her laugh sounded like twigs snapping.

Barley didn't know what else to do. His hands trembled as he opened the gate. It banged shut behind him, making him jump. He crossed the yard slowly, then ducked through the door into the dark little hut.

TWO

Somewhere else in the forest, inside of Lost Castle, Rye sat on a pile of old sacks in the corner of the kitchen next to a mound of mostly-rotten potatoes. Some of the potatoes were so bad that bubbly white juice burst from their skins the moment he touched them. He scrunched his nose and hunted for a potato good enough to be worth cutting up. As he searched, he thought about Barley safe at home in bed with his stomach full of supper. At least Rye hoped Barley was home safe in bed. Of course he was. Barley wouldn't have tried to follow the brigands. He wouldn't be wandering around in the forest right now, alone, in the dark.

Then again, maybe Barley had tried to follow the brigands. Rye knew Barley was brave, and he didn't always think things through before he did them. Worried, Rye stared at the tiny, dark window high in the kitchen wall and hoped with all his heart that his brother had gone home.

Beside him, Jep dropped the squishy half of a potato in a bucket and the good half in a large, cracked bowl. "They stole these potatoes months ago," Jep said. "But they're too lazy to go out and get fresh ones. They're the laziest brigands in the entire kingdom. This should be called Lazy Castle, if you ask me."

"No one's asking you," Tildy said, a spoon in her hand and her fists on her hips. "Hurry up. If I don't start the soup soon, they'll lock us in the dungeon tonight!"

Rye and Jep found a few more potatoes to put in the bowl, then took it to where Tildy had a big pot of water boiling over the fire.

"Now what?" Rye asked.

"Now we get the bowls and cups ready, then when the soup's done we serve everyone in the dining hall. After they eat, if there's any left over, we can eat. Then we scrub the kitchen, then wash all their clothes and clean their boots, and if it isn't morning yet, we can sleep for a bit."

Rye wondered why brigands who were too lazy to keep themselves clean needed their clothes washed every night. "You say we have to clean their boots?" Rye asked.

"Yes," Tildy said, and pinched her nose. "And it's horrible. They never do watch what they're stepping in!"

Rye glanced back at the pile of rotten potatoes with a grin. "Oh, we'll clean their boots tonight. We most certainly will. Listen, everyone, I have a plan."

THREE

Inside the old woman's hut, Barley's head almost touched the ceiling. A fireplace, a pile of old blankets, and a little table with a single, crooked chair filled the tiny room. Cupboards with doors falling off their hinges hung crazily from the walls.

"Help yourself. I've already eaten." The old woman pointed to a plate of bread and cheese on the table.

"Thank you." Barley sat down in the rickety chair. His stomach reminded him he hadn't eaten anything but blackberries since breakfast. He carefully picked up the bread. It was soft and smelled like honey. He took a small nibble, then a big bite. Without realizing it, he ate the whole loaf, then started on the cheese.

While Barely ate, the old woman dug around under the pile of blankets.

"Aha! Here it is!" She dragged out something long and heavy, covered in cloth and wound around with string. "I've been waiting a long time to give this to someone." She heaved it up and set it on the table with a thunk.

"What is it?" Barley asked.

"See for yourself," the old woman said.

Barley untied the string. His fingers tingled as he unwrapped the cloth. His heart thumped, this time with excitement. It was a sword!

The sword lit up the room with its mirror-bright blade. On the hilt, jewels sparkled in all the colors of the rainbow.

"You've been waiting to give this to someone?" Barley asked, not daring to hope that it might be for him.

"I have. I'll loan it to you, if you can use it," the old woman said.

Barley sighed. The sword was longer than he was tall. He'd never be able to lift it. Besides, he'd played with the toy wooden swords his father had made for him and Rye, but he didn't know how to use a real one. "I don't think I can," Barley said.

"Maybe you can, and maybe you can't. Let's give it a little test. Put your hand on the hilt, just like that, yes, that's right."

Barley wrapped his fingers around the handle of the sword.

"Now answer my question. Why are you here?"

"Because I want to help my brother," Barley said. The sword shuddered a tiny bit, then lay still. Surprised, Barley almost let go. Then he gripped harder.

"And why do you want to do that?" the old woman asked, her eyes on the sword.

"Because...because it's my fault he got caught!"

The old woman shook her head. "Ah, a guilty conscience then. That won't do. You're going to help your brother because it will make you feel better. Try again. Why do you want to help your brother?"

"Because if no one rescues him, I'll never see him again!" Barley said.

"Oh, so you're going to miss him? That's too bad." The old woman wrung her hands and pretended to sniffle a little. Then she gripped the table and put her long nose right in

Barley's face. "It's still all about you, though, isn't it, my boy? One last try. Why do you want to help your brother?"

Angry that the old woman seemed to be making fun of him, Barley stood up. "Because he's been taken to Lost Castle! They'll make him their slave, and never let him come home."

"So maybe you want to help him because he's in trouble?" the old woman asked.

"Yes!" Barley said. The sword hummed.

The old woman clapped her hands. "You want to help him because he's unhappy. He's trapped, and he can't get back home on his own."

Barley thought about how sad and afraid Rye must be feeling, and his heart longed to help him. The sword sprang up from the table and lifted itself into the air.

"That's it! You've got it!" The old woman hopped on one foot and waved her spindly arms in triumph.

Excited, Barley swung the sword and accidentally knocked a cupboard door off its hinges.

"Careful there!" the old woman croaked. "Save that for the Lord of Lost Castle."

"I'm sorry!" Barley's excitement turned to embarrassment, and the sword grew heavy. The tip of the blade thunked to the floor while Barley gripped the handle tightly to keep from dropping it. "Wait, what should I save for the Lord of Lost Castle?"

"The swinging and the chopping!" The old woman picked up the cupboard door and hung it back on upside-down. "The fighting and the felling!"

Barley stared at his reflection in the blade. His puzzled face stared back at him as clear as if he were looking in a pool of still water. "How did I lift it?"

"When this sword is held by one with an unselfish heart it has a magical power. No enemy can stand against it. So long as you use it to help others it will fight your battles for you. But if you should use it to serve yourself, its magic will be gone." The old woman leaned closer. "I want you to use it to defeat the Lord of Lost Castle."

Barley dropped the sword. The hilt hit the floor with a bang. He didn't want to fight the Lord of Lost Castle. He only wanted to find the castle. Once he found it, he could tell everyone in the village. They could tell the king. The king could send his soldiers to free Rye and all the other children that the Lord of Lost Castle had captured. Fighting wasn't supposed to be Barley's job.

"I don't know how to fight," Barley said.

"I told you, the sword will fight for you!"

"Then why don't you use it?" Barley asked.

"Because I'm a selfish old woman!" she said. "I want to see the Lord of Lost Castle defeated out of spite and wicked vengeance!" The old woman danced a jig once around the room, then collapsed in a heap on top of the blankets. While lying on her back, she said, "That's my castle he's living in, you know. He stole it from me, and I want it back! They used to call me the Witch of Lost Castle. Now I'm just the Lost Witch. Because I lost. I lost my Lost Castle..." Her voice faded.

Barley waited for her to say more. Instead, she started to snore.

"Excuse me?" Barley asked.

"What?" the old woman sat up. "Oh, yes, the sword. I can't use it to fight the Lord of Lost Castle because I would be doing it for myself. You, on the other hand, are doing it to help your brother. So you will succeed where I would fail."

She yawned. "Now get some sleep. You have a long day tomorrow." The old woman lay down and started to snore.

Barley sat in the chair, wondering where he was supposed to sleep. At last he took one of the blankets from the edge of the pile where the old woman lay and curled up on the floor by the fireplace. The thought of fighting the terrible Lord of Lost Castle and all his brigands frightened him, but if what the witch had said about the magic sword was true, he might be able to do it. Then he could rescue Rye and their friends from Humble Village who had been taken by the brigands.

In the fading firelight, the sword gleamed on the knotty old boards of the cottage floor. Barley reached out his hand to touch the sword's handle. It quivered under his fingers.

Barley decided he would try.

FOUR

The next morning the brigands of Lost Castle woke up to find their usual, neatly folded pile of clothes and a clean-looking pair of boots beside their beds. The unsatisfying smell of porridge with not quite enough salt in it filled the air, making them hungry and grumpy. In no hurry, they fumbled into their clothes, growling and scratching. When the castle bell rang to let them know breakfast was ready, they each put one foot in one boot...

...and shrieked in surprise.

Feet came out of boots faster than anyone would have guessed those lazy brigands could move. Toes dripped with yellow slime and wriggling maggots. A terrible smell filled the room. One brigand threw his boot at the wall, but hit another brigand in the face instead. Rotten potato slime sprayed everywhere. The brigand who had been hit yelped and threw a boot back at the first one, but missed. The boot landed on a third brigand's head, where it dripped potato slime into his hair and ears. Soon all the brigands were yelling and fighting each other. Even the two brigands who had been on night watch ran in to see what was going on.

No one noticed the five children creeping across the courtyard to the castle gate.

Tom Cobbler pulled on the gate lever while the other four each grabbed one of the spokes that stuck out from the wheel that would raise the iron bars. A fat chain wrapped around the wheel and ran up to a hole in the wall. The lever went "clunk," and the chain rattled. It pulled tight when all the children tried to turn the wheel, but it didn't move. Rye ran around to the other side of the wheel and pushed up on a spoke. When Tom joined him, the wheel gradually began to move, and so did the gate. It raised up one inch, and then another.

"The slaves are escaping!" boomed a terrible voice from across the courtyard.

There, in the arch of a doorway, stood the Lord of Lost Castle. Instead of ragged leather trousers and a tattered shirt like his brigands, he wore a suit of fine velvet. The jeweled crown on his head was too small for him and so sat a little bit crooked in his oily black curls. A deep frown pulled the dangling corners of his moustache down even farther. He glared at the children. The polished boot in his hand dripped rotten potato slime onto the ground.

"HEAVE!" shouted the children all together. The gate raised up another inch.

"STOP THEM!" the Lord of Lost Castle bellowed. "Get out here and STOP THEM!"

Reluctant in their bare, slimy feet, the brigands of Lost Castle hobbled out into the courtyard. When they saw the children trying to turn the gate wheel they hobbled faster.

"Janet, you're the smallest," Rye said with a glance at the gate. "Can you squeeze underneath?"

Janet let go of the wheel and ran for the gate, but one of the brigands reached her first. He caught her around the waist and lifted her high in the air. Other brigands pried the rest of the children off the gate wheel and dragged them across the courtyard until they were all standing in front of the Lord of Lost Castle.

"It seems to me that you little runts haven't done a good job of teaching our new slave how things are done around here." The Lord of Lost Castle sneered at the children. "Perhaps some time in the dungeon will give you a chance to explain it to him."

All the children except for Rye began to beg and plead, "No, please, not again! Not the dungeon!"

"Wait," Rye said. "It was my idea. You don't have to...please don't punish them!"

"To the dungeon with them all!" the Lord of Lost Castle shouted. Before Rye could say another word, growling brigands pushed, shoved, and carried them all toward a dark little opening at the base of one of the crumbling towers.

Rough hands on his shoulders shoved Rye toward the dungeon door. Janet, usually quiet and shy, screamed and kicked and howled, "No! Not the dungeon!" The brigand carrying her hardly flinched as he disappeared into the dark doorway. Tom Cobbler hung his head and Jep shot Rye a spiteful look as they were pushed in. Rye stumbled through the doorway after them, helpless against the iron hands clamped tightly on his shoulders, ashamed, miserable, and frightened. Rye's first try at escaping had not gone very well.

FIVE

Right about then, the old witch led Barley through the forest. She chuckled to herself and sang, "No enemy can stand against it! No enemy can stand against it! Remember that—it's very important. No enemy can stand against it!"

Barley carried the sword with him as they walked. It felt light in his hand, almost as if it were carrying him. He was beginning to feel that with this magic sword, he couldn't lose. He would defeat the Lord of Lost Castle, rescue his brother and the other children, and then they would all go back to the village. He would be a hero!

The sword fell to the ground with a clunk. The old woman spun around, an angry gleam in her eye.

"What were you thinking about, young man?" she asked.

"I was thinking about rescuing my brother," Barley said.

"Oh?" the old woman put her hands on her hips. "Is that all?"

Barley hung his head. "No. I was thinking of becoming a hero because I'd rescued everyone." The sword dragged in the dirt. Barley tried to lift it, but his arms weren't strong enough. Barley gasped. "Did I ruin it? Is the magic gone?" Tears pricked his eyes.

"Think about your brother," the old woman said.

Barley imagined Rye trapped in Lost Castle, forced to work as a slave. His heart ached for him. He had to rescue him, and all the other children too.

The sword lifted from the ground.

"So long as you are thinking of others and not of yourself, the sword will serve you," the old woman warned. "Remember that."

"But what if I can't? What if I forget?" Barley asked.

"I know you can do it. You saved that baby deer. That means you know how to think of others before yourself."

Barley nodded. He would try. He had to if he was going to save Rye. Carrying the sword high, and careful to keep his mind on his true goal, he followed the old witch through the trees.

END of Episode Two

EPISODE THREE: THE BATTLE OF LOST CASTLE

ONE

Not even the tiniest glimmer of light shone in the dungeon cell where Rye sat on the cold, damp floor. The other children huddled around him. In the darkness, things hissed and squeaked and scrabbled. Something crawled over Rye's foot. He kicked it away with a shout.

"How long do you think we'll have to stay down here this time?" Tildy asked in a teary voice.

"They're awful mad," said Jep, shaky and cross. "Maybe they'll never let us out."

"I'm sorry," Rye said. "I thought…"

"You thought one of your tricks would help us escape?" Jep asked. "Well it didn't!"

Rye put his head down on his knees and curled himself up tighter. He'd been trying to help, but all he'd done was get everyone in trouble.

No one said anything for a while. Then Tom Cobbler giggled. "The brigands did look funny."

"With rotten potato slime all over them," Janet added.

Rye smiled a little. "They did, didn't they?"

"I'm hungry," Jep said.

The children fell silent.

"I wish we were at home," Tildy said.

"What's the village like, Rye?" Tom Cobbler asked. "Tell us. I can hardly remember it."

"Yes, tell us!" the others said.

Rye closed his eyes. It didn't make a bit of difference with the cell so dark, but it seemed easier to see the village in his mind with his eyes closed. "There's a road, and a well, and houses with daubed walls and thatched roofs. There's fields all around, and gardens, and apple trees. You can hear sheep bells, and cow bells, and the smith's hammer, and the mill wheel creaking..."

As Rye spoke, even the rats grew quiet to listen. Every word made the children sadder, made them long for home even more, but they didn't want Rye to stop.

Two

Barley stood at the rim of a deep valley. The pointed tops of four towers rose above the trees ahead. Moss covered the crooked shingles, making them nearly the same color as the leaves.

"There it is boy. You can meet me here with the sword when you're done." The old woman sat down on a rock. "Go on now."

"You're not coming with me?" Barley asked.

"Certainly not! Shoo, shoo, be on your way! Remember, an unselfish heart, and no enemy can stand against you. You've nothing to be afraid of." She hugged herself and stomped her feet. "I'm glad I'm not the Lord of Lost Castle today! Hee hee!"

THREE

No road, not even a track, led to the front gate of Lost Castle. Quietly, Barley crept forward through the trees for a better look. Two brigands leaned against the wall outside the front gate, each one with a long spear at his side. More brigands moved around in the open courtyard beyond the gate. A magic sword was a good thing to have, but how could he fight so many men? A tingle of fear crawled up his back.

Barley thought about going back and telling the old witch that he wouldn't do it, but then he thought of his brother. Rye was trapped in that castle. No turning back now. Barley raised his sword.

"This is new," one of the brigands said when he saw Barley marching up to the gate all alone, carrying a sword nearly as long as he was tall.

"I get the sword," said the second one.

"Only if you grab him first." The first brigand lunged at Barley.

The sword swung itself through the air, dragging Barley's arm along with it. It knocked the first brigand's spear from his hands. Terrified, the man turned and ran into the forest. The other brigand ran into the castle, shouting, "Close the gates! Close the gates!"

Barley ran after him. The big metal gate above him creaked down. It had spikes on the bottom like long teeth.

Barley covered his head with one arm. The sword flew forward, towing Barley under the gate just before it clanged to the ground.

Dozens of brigands stood in the courtyard. Some drew knives and swords while others raised clubs and shields.

The magic sword charged forward, swinging right and left. Barley had to hop and dance to keep up with it. Weapons clattered to the ground, knocked from the brigands' hands. Angry shouts turned to frightened cries as the brigands realized none of them could fight Barley's magic sword.

"Open the gate! Open the gate!" they began to yell. The gate cranked open enough for them to wiggle out underneath. Barley chased them, swinging the sword as he went.

Barley leapt in front of one brigand who hadn't reached the gate yet and aimed the sword at his face. "Where are the children?"

"In the dungeon," the frightened brigand said.

"How do I get there?" Barley asked.

The brigand pointed to a door. Barley let him go and ran across the courtyard. The big iron door had a lock on it. Barley rattled the door, but it wouldn't open. He tried hitting it with the sword, but nothing happened.

FOUR

"WHAT'S GOING ON OUT HERE?"

Barley turned to see a man with a tangled black beard, mean black eyes, and a small jeweled crown in his black hair. The man stood on the opposite side of the courtyard at the bottom of a staircase.

It could only be the Lord of Lost Castle.

"I've come for my brother," Barley shouted, not afraid at all. His magic sword had chased away all the brigands, and the Lord of Lost Castle would be no different. "Give me the key to the dungeon."

"I have the key here," said the Lord of Lost Castle. He pulled a large key on a ring from a hook on his belt. "Come and get it."

To Barley's surprise, the Lord of Lost Castle sat down on the stairs.

"You want this key, don't you?" the Lord of Lost Castle jangled the key in the air.

Barley took a step forward, but then stopped. This was a trick. The Lord of Lost Castle was sitting there, waiting for Barley to come and get the key. It had to be a trick.

"Think of how famous you'll be, single-handedly defeating the Lord of Lost Castle. You want that, don't you?"

Barley swallowed hard. He thought of his brother. He had come to rescue his brother. That's all. He didn't care about being famous. He'd already found out that the sword wouldn't work if he thought of becoming a famous hero.

The Lord of Lost Castle raised his black eyebrows. "You're angry at me, aren't you? For stealing your brother. For taking your friends. You'd like to get back at me for it, wouldn't you?" The Lord of Lost Castle smiled.

Anger flashed in Barley's chest, burning like fire. He ran forward, but the sword clanged to the ground. Barley raised it, but his arms shook. He tried to point the sword at the Lord of Lost Castle, but it was so heavy he could barely hold it.

The Lord of Lost Castle chuckled. He drew his own sword and stood up.

"I'm here for my brother!" Barley shouted. "I'm here to help him, and all of my friends!"

The sword grew light again in Barley's hands.

The Lord of Lost Castle scowled. He sat down.

"Give me the key," Barley demanded.

"Never." the Lord of Lost Castle raised his sword, but this time he did not get up from where he sat on the stairs.

Barley ran forward and swung the sword, expecting to knock the blade from the Lord of Lost Castle's hand. Instead, the Lord of Lost Castle met his blow. Barley felt a jolt as the two swords collided. He stepped back and swung again. This time the Lord of Lost Castle blocked, then leaned forward and slashed at Barley, all while sitting on the steps. Confused, Barley stumbled back.

He heard the voice of the old woman singing in his head. "No enemy can stand against it!" But if that were true, then why couldn't the sword defeat the Lord of Lost Castle?

Then Barley realized something. The Lord of Lost Castle wasn't standing. He was sitting.

What if the magic only worked when his enemy was standing?

Barley took a step back. "Stand up and fight."

The Lord of Lost Castle laughed. "I know that sword." He shook his head. "She thought she could send a child into my castle to defeat me with a magic sword? I know how the magic works, boy. It won't harm me."

Breathing hard, Barley took another step back. Unless the Lord of Lost Castle stood up to fight, there was no way for Barley to win.

"Ah, now you're afraid, aren't you?" the Lord of Lost Castle said. "You're afraid you'll fail. Afraid I'll take your sword and throw you down in the dungeon with the others. Afraid for yourself. You should be. My men are lazy cowards, but they'll be back soon enough, and by then I'll have that sword to hang on my wall where it belongs, and this castle will be mine forever! And so will you."

Barley was afraid, but he wasn't afraid for himself. He was afraid he wouldn't be able to rescue his brother. He had to think of a way to get the Lord of Lost Castle to stand up.

The Lord of Lost Castle had stood up once before, once when Barley couldn't use the sword because he was thinking of himself. The sword's magic was working now, but Barley could pretend that it wasn't working!

Barley took another step back and swung the sword down. The blade hit the ground with a heavy clang. Barley grunted, pretending to try and lift it. The sword trembled, fighting Barley, wanting to rise into the air. Barley kept it down.

The Lord of Lost Castle sprang from the steps with a shout of triumph and raised his sword high over Barley's head. The sword in Barley's hand leapt up. It wrenched the weapon from the Lord of Lost's Castle's hand, then pointed at his throat.

"Give me the key!" Barley said.

The Lord of Lost Castle stared, amazed and afraid.

"Drop the key, now!" Barley shouted.

The Lord of Lost Castle dropped the key on the ground.

"Now go," Barley said. "Leave this place, and never return."

The magic sword hummed as if in warning.

With fear and anger in his eyes, the Lord of Lost Castle glared at Barley. Then he turned toward the castle gate. Barley followed him across the courtyard.

The Lord of Lost Castle took two steps, then lunged for one of the swords that his brigands had dropped. His fingers had just curled around the grip when Barley's magic sword slammed down on the blade. With a yelp of surprise, the Lord of Lost Castle jerked his hand back. The magic sword whistled through the air, knocking the crown from the Lord of Lost Castle's head. The Lord of Lost Castle flattened himself to avoid the blow. Scrambling to his feet, the Lord of Lost Castle ran with the sword slashing behind him. He ran all the way to the gate, then dove for the narrow opening underneath. With a final slash, the sword sliced off the bottoms of his boots just as his feet slid safely out of its reach.

With the tops of his boots flapping uselessly over his socks, the Lord of Lost Castle ran off into the forest. He shouted for his men. Barley looked at the chain that worked the castle gate, wondering if he could figure out how to close it. He didn't want the Lord of Lost Castle and his men to get back in.

The shouts and sounds of flapping boot tops came to a sudden stop. Wondering what had happened, Barley looked back out the front gate. The Lord of Lost Castle was nowhere in sight. Not only that, instead of thick trees at the bottom of a shady valley, he saw a meadow filled with wildflowers. The view out the castle gate had entirely changed.

Barley walked up to the bars and stared out, searching for any sign of the valley he'd climbed down into earlier that morning. He couldn't tell which direction it might be in. He didn't know how he would find the witch that he'd left at the valley's edge.

At least the Lord of Lost Castle wasn't anywhere in sight.

FIVE

Barley went to the place where the Lord of Lost Castle had dropped the key. He would worry about what had happened to the valley later. First he had to find Rye and the others. He picked up the key and ran to the dungeon door, unlocked it, and climbed down a long, dark, winding staircase. When it got so dark he couldn't see anything, Barley stopped, afraid to go any further.

"Hello!" Barley shouted.

"Hello?" someone called back.

Barley's eyes began to adjust to the dark. Ahead of him, dim faces peered from behind heavy iron bars.

"Is Rye here?" Barley said.

"Here!" A hand stuck through the bars and waved. "Barley! Is that you?"

Barley ran down the last few steps. He dropped the sword and put the key in the lock.

"How did you find me? Is that a sword? How did you get the key?" Rye asked.

"It's Barley! He found us! We're escaping!" Excited whispers filled the air.

"Quiet! The brigands!" Rye hissed.

"They're gone," Barley said. "The Lord of Lost Castle and all his men are gone."

"Hooray!" the children shouted.

Barley swung the door open and stood back as a flood of children poured up the stairs.

"Where did you get that sword?" Rye stared at the shiny blade. Even in the dim light at the bottom of the dungeon stairs, it glimmered.

"The Witch of Lost Castle loaned it to me. It's magic! It fought off all the brigands, and the Lord of Lost Castle too. I just had to hold it, and swish, swish, swish, whoops!" Pretending to swing the sword in the air, Barley lost his balance and toppled against the stairs.

"That's amazing," Rye said. He helped Barley up, then hugged him tight. "Are you all right?"

"I'm all right." Barley said, but he didn't feel all right. He was tired, and he wasn't sure how they were going to get home. He bent down to pick up the sword, but it wouldn't move. For some reason, the magic wasn't working anymore. Maybe, Barley thought, it was because he was thinking about how tired he was, but he was too tired to care. Rye bent down to help him, and with the two of them working together they were able to drag the sword up the stairs.

Up in the courtyard, Tom and Jep were playing with the weapons that the brigands had left behind. Barley checked the gate and saw the meadow on the other side. That probably meant they were safe from the Lord of Lost Castle. That was good, but since he didn't know how to find the witch, he wasn't sure what to do next.

Janet asked, "Can we go home now?" as if she didn't dare to believe it.

"No one's here to stop us!" said Rye.

Barley shook his head, exhausted. "I don't know which way to go. When I got here, the castle was in a valley, but now it's in a meadow."

"It does that," Tom said. "It never stays in the same place for more than a few days."

"There are provisions in the castle," Rye said. "Let's get some food before we go. Don't worry, we'll find our way home somehow."

The children raided the castle pantries, crying out with joy at the apples and cheeses and sausages they had never been allowed to eat. They ate all that they wanted and loaded up sacks with the rest.

"Where are the servants and cooks and everyone?" Barley asked as they gathered in the courtyard.

"No servants. We did all the work in the castle," Rye said.

"Thank you for rescuing us." Tildy put her arms around Barley and hugged him tight.

"Yes, thank you, thank you!" they all cheered.

A pounding on the castle gate cut the cheering short. Determined to protect his brother and their friends, Barley picked up the sword from where he and Rye had left it. This time it sprang up in his hand. "Who's there?" he shouted.

"Let me in!" croaked the old witch. "It's my castle, after all!"

The other children stared, frightened, at the old woman who scowled at them from the far side of the gate.

"She's the one who loaned me the sword," Barley said. "She's a friend."

"Open the gate a little wider, please!" the old woman said. "I don't feel like crawling in over my own front doorstep."

With Barley's help, the children turned the crank and raised the gate high.

"Thank you very much!" the Witch of Lost Castle said as she walked through the gate. She stumped over to where the crown lay on the ground, picked it up, and planted it in her tangled gray hair. She patted it in place with her bony fingers, then turned around and asked the children, "How do I look?"

None of them dared to answer. The crown didn't exactly match her tattered black dress and shawl, but they weren't about to tell her that.

The witch crossed her spindly ankles and made a creaky little curtsey to Barley. "Thank you, brave warrior, for liberating Lost Castle. If you will please kindly return my magic sword."

"Oh," said Barley. Now that the adventure was over, he found he didn't want to give the sword up. The moment he thought about how much he wanted to keep it, it grew heavier in his hand until the tip rested on the ground. A little sheepishly, Barley held out the handle to the witch.

"If you should ever need to borrow it again, only come and ask me," the witch gave Barley a wink as she took the sword.

"Can you tell us the way home?" Barley asked.

"That depends on where you live," the old woman said.

"Humble Village," Rye said. "Do you know how to get there?"

"That's easy! Follow the sun to the river, then follow the river to the bridge, then follow the bridge to the village," the old woman said. "You'll be there before sundown tomorrow."

Six

The children struck out across the meadow, following the afternoon sun. They crossed the forest, reached the river by sunset, ate food from their sacks, and then sat around a big campfire they built themselves. The children begged Barley for the whole story, so he told them how he helped the baby deer and found the old woman who loaned him the magic sword. Then he told them how he fought off the guards and chased away the Lord of Lost Castle. When the story was over, they all fell asleep around the campfire on the soft, dry sand by the side of the river.

In the morning they hiked along the river as it wound past the forest. It went around the edge of the rocks and traced the rim of Grayfallow Swamp.

"The bridge! The bridge!"

"I saw it first!"

"No, I saw it!"

The other children ran ahead. By the time Barley and Rye crossed the bridge and reached the village, everyone had come out of their houses. People were shouting and crying and laughing all at once. Parents picked up their lost children and danced around the village green, carrying them on their shoulders and in their arms.

"Barley! Rye!" Barley's mother and father ran toward them. Mother smothered them with hugs and kisses.

"We were worried sick!" Mother said.

"You brought the others back with you!" Father's eyes shone with pride.

"Barley did it," Rye said. "He rescued us from Lost Castle."

"I had some help," Barley said.

"But you were the hero," Rye said.

Barley smiled. "Maybe this time. But next time, you can rescue me."

END of Episode Three

Episode Four: Heroes in Training

ONE

That night the whole village put on a feast to celebrate the children who had come home. They hung glowing lanterns under a tent in the village square and filled the tables with puddings, stews, and pies. After everyone ate as much as they could hold, Barley told the story of how he had rescued his brother and their friends from Lost Castle.

Rye thought about interrupting to add that he and all the other children had put rotten potatoes in the brigands' boots, but then he remembered it was the reason everyone had been thrown in the dungeon. He decided to leave the storytelling to Barley.

After the story, Soldier Jack took out his fiddle and played the one tune he knew while everyone else pushed back the tables and danced. At last the bright moon sank behind the Red Mountains and everyone headed off to bed. As soon as Barley and Rye came in the house, their mother gave them a fierce scolding for running off across the river when she had plainly told them not to. Then she hugged them both, cried again, and thanked Barley for rescuing his brother and all the other children.

As tired as he was from the feasting and dancing, Rye couldn't sleep that night. He knew he shouldn't have let Barley cross the river that day when the brigands came. On the other hand, if he hadn't, then Tom, Jep, Tildy, and Janet would still be scrubbing floors, peeling rotten potatoes, and cleaning boots for the brigands of Lost Castle. If it hadn't been for Rye's quick thinking when the brigands showed up, Barley would have been caught by the brigands too. Both Barley and Rye would have been carried off to Lost Castle together. Then there would have been no rescue, no magic sword, none of it would have happened.

And yet Barley was getting all the attention. It wasn't that Rye was jealous. He didn't want all the attention for himself. He only wanted a little bit. Barley could share a little of the glory, couldn't he?

Two

The next morning, their father told Barley and Rye that they could have an entire day off from chores.

They had just sat down to their favorite porridge for breakfast when Jep and Tildy Weaver showed up at the door, along with their smiling parents. The Weavers thanked Barley for rescuing their children and gave him a new woolen blanket.

"Come out and play as soon as you can!" Jep said as the Weavers left.

While mother exclaimed over the blanket and father beamed, Rye stirred his porridge. It had been terribly nice of the Weavers to give Barley a new blanket. His old one was patched and ragged, it was true, but so was Rye's. Rye wondered if things would be different if his plan to help everyone escape Lost Castle had worked out. Then he'd be the one everyone was proud of.

As the boys headed out the door to enjoy their day off, Tom Cobbler arrived with his father and mother. Tom's mother burst into tears and threw her arms around Barley, thanking him for rescuing Tom. Then Tom's father gave Barley a new pair of shoes.

"We're going to the meadow to play," Tom said. "You'll come, won't you?"

"Be right there," Barley said.

Mother and Father thanked the Cobblers and waved to them as they walked away. Barley sat down, pulled off his old shoes, and tried on his new ones. "These fit nice!" He said, wiggling his toes.

Rye glanced down and noticed how easy it was to see his own big toe through the hole in the top of his shoe. He told himself that it was a good thing that Barley had a pair of new shoes. Since Barley had new shoes now, Mother and Father might buy Rye a pair too. But it wasn't the shoes that were bothering him, not really.

As soon as Barley had his new shoes on, he charged out the door. "Race you to the meadow, Rye!" he said. Rye didn't feel like running, so he was still in the yard when Janet Grover arrived with her parents, each of them carrying an armload of wood.

"Is Barley here?" Janet asked shyly.

"He's gone to the meadow to play," Rye said.

"We'd like to thank your brother for rescuing Janet," said Janet's mother. "Will you tell him for us?"

"This is for your family." Janet's father nodded to the wood in his arms. "Can we put it down over there?" He glanced at the woodpile in the corner of the yard.

"Thank you," Rye said, remembering his manners. "Can I take that for you, Janet?"

Janet nodded and stared at the ground while Rye took the wood from her and carried it to the pile. At least, Rye thought, this wood wasn't just for Barley. This would save him from having to chop some wood later too. He started to feel a little better.

"It's a good thing Barley came for us," Janet said. "If not, we could still be in that dungeon. Sometimes they left us in there for days."

Rye had started to feel a little better, but now he felt worse. It had been his fault that the children had been put in the dungeon. Of course, it was only because he'd been trying to help them all escape.

"No need to hang about here, children," Rye's mother said. "Run along to the meadow and play."

"Yes, go on," Janet's mother said.

Janet dashed out of the gate as fast as she could go. Rye followed slowly behind.

THREE

By the time Rye reached the meadow, all the other children were playing a game that looked like a contest to see how ridiculous they could be while Barley chased them around, waving his toy wooden sword in the air.

"Hey, Rye!" Barley shouted when he saw him. Barley sounded very happy to see him, as if he'd been anxious for Rye to arrive.

"Hello," Rye shouted back, feeling hopeful. Maybe Barley wanted to play the part where the brigands came to capture them, and then Rye could help him hide.

"Do you want to be the Lord of Lost Castle?" Barley shouted back.

So much for that. "No, thank you," Rye said. "I think I'll just go sit in the dungeon."

"What did you say?" Barley shouted.

"No thanks! I'm going to the dungeon!" Rye said.

"If that's what you want. It's right over there." Barley pointed to a bush. Then Barley chased Jep Weaver while Jep hopped, twirled, and hooted in a hilarious impression of a terrified brigand that made all the other children laugh.

Rye sat in the shade beside the bush and picked at the strands of grass by his feet. It wasn't fair. He couldn't see why everyone was making so much fuss about Barley. It really hadn't been Barley that had rescued them at all. It had been that magic sword.

All the other children came running. They piled into the shade under the bush. Rye scowled as they crowded around him.

"Oh help, we're in the dungeon!" squeaked Molly Baker, who hadn't even been there. What did she know about it?

"We'll be eaten by the terrible rats!" Tildy Weaver wailed.

The children all whimpered and moaned. Rye rolled his eyes.

"I'll save you!" Barley marched up to where the children sat under the bush. He pretended to unlock an imaginary cell door with an imaginary key. "You're all free!"

"Hooray!" the children shouted, all except Rye. They jumped up and ran out into the meadow, all except Rye.

"Let's play again!"

"Who wants to be the witch this time?"

"I'll be the Lord of Lost Castle," Jep said. He put a scowl on his face and struck a bold pose that made everyone giggle.

"Hey, Rye, you're free," Barley said. "You can come out of the dungeon now."

"Huzzah," Rye said. He got up, brushed himself off, and stalked out of the meadow with his hands stuck in his pockets.

FOUR

The next morning, Rye woke long before dawn. He slipped out of his cot, silent as a ghost, and crept the two steps over to the other side of the loft where Barley slept. Bending down, he felt around on the floor in the dark until his fingers brushed soft, new leather. Barley's new shoes were in Rye's hands in a wink. Rye tip-toed down the stairs with the shoes, trying to think of a good place to hide them. He thought about stuffing them up the chimney, but then settled on the butter churn. After tucking them down inside and silently setting the lid and the churning stick in place, he tip-toed back to bed.

"Where are my new shoes, Rye?" Barley stood over him, gold hair blazing in the morning sun that beamed through the small, open window.

Rye squinted up at him, then moaned and rolled over. "How should I know?"

"Because you hid them. Where are they?" He sounded furious.

"It wasn't me." Rye pulled the covers over his head. "It was the pixies."

"There's no such thing as pixies," Barley said.

"Sure there are," Rye said from under his blanket. "Last month they stole your old shoes and hid them in the washtub, and two weeks ago they stole your socks and hid them in the rafters, and last Tuesday they stole the milking bucket and balanced it on top of the chimney." He tried not to giggle. It was very, very hard.

"That was you every time," Barley said, "and we both know it."

Rye peeked at him from under the blanket. Always in the past, when Rye had hidden something belonging to Barley and told him the pixies had done it, Barley had run around the house with Rye, laughing, trying to find the thing that the pixies had stolen. It had been one of their favorite games.

"Ma! Rye stole my shoes!" Barley called down the ladder.

"Stop being such a baby." Rye pitched his pillow at Barley's head.

Barley caught the pillow and whirled on Rye. "Was it a baby who rescued you from Lost Castle?" he demanded.

"No." Rye sat up straight in bed. "It was a magic sword."

"And I didn't have anything to do with it?" Barley threw his hands in the air.

"No, you didn't." Rye jumped up out of bed. With both boys on their feet now, Rye, only two inches taller, glared slightly down at him, "You don't even know how to use a sword!"

"Well, neither do you," Barley said.

"Anyone could have done it so long as they had that magic sword," Rye said.

"The witch chose me!" Barley said.

"Not because you were special or anything. It was because you just happened to show up. And you happened to show up because I let the brigands take me while you were hiding in a blackberry bush!"

"I came looking for you!" Barley shouted.

"And what were you going to do if you found me? You would have been caught too if you hadn't had that magic sword, which you didn't even know how to use."

"I knew how to use it. You just had to think of other people and not of yourself."

"That was the magic. I meant you don't know how to fight with a sword. There's no one in this whole entire village who knows anything at all about sword fighting."

"You're wrong there, Rye," Father said.

The boys turned to see Father watching them from where he stood on the ladder to the loft. Rye started to say that Barley most certainly was not a real fighter, but Father spoke first.

"There is someone in the village who knows about sword fighting," Father said.

"Who?" Barley asked.

"Maybe he'd teach the two of you, if you'd ask him," Father said.

"It's Soldier Jack, isn't it?" Rye asked, wondering why he'd never thought of this before.

"Yes. And if you'll stop arguing long enough to eat breakfast and do your chores, you can go over and see him when morning work is done," Father said.

"Hooray!" shouted Barley. "We're going to learn to be real heroes now!"

FIVE

The missing shoes forgotten, Barley slid down the ladder, with Rye close behind. Excited, the boys rushed through breakfast and hurried to do their chores. Rye was certain he'd be better at sword fighting than Barley and then they'd see who was a real hero.

"What's all the hurry, boys?" Mother asked when the basket of eggs Barley had tossed onto the table nearly slid off and the milk almost sloshed out of the bucket Rye swung into her hands.

"We're going to be adventuring heroes!" Barley said.

"You play that game every day," Mother chuckled.

"No, we're going to be real heroes," Barley said. "We're going to ask Soldier Jack to teach us how to fight with swords."

"Oh really, now?" Mother asked. "Haven't you had enough adventuring?"

"No, we're just getting started." Barley grinned.

"Go and fetch the water now," Mother said.

"And then can we go?" Barley asked.

"Yes, then you can go."

Barley and Rye each took a pair of empty buckets to the well. They had only begun to fill them when a horrible shriek came from the house.

Even Father came running from the field. He reached the door about the same time as Barley and Rye. There stood Mother in the doorway, her face red and angry. In each hand she held a white, dripping shoe.

"Who put Barley's new shoes in the butter churn?" Mother roared.

Everyone stared at Rye. Rye just blinked at the shoes. He hadn't meant for them to stay in the butter churn this long. He had thought Barley would surely find them before breakfast.

"Ah," Barley said solemnly. "It must have been the pixies."

SIX

Rye rinsed the cream from Barley's new shoes by dunking them in a bucket of water, then dried them off as best he could using the bottom edge of his long shirt. He used another bucketful to clean out Mother's butter churn. Barley waited, standing in his soggy shoes, while Rye put the rinsed-out butter churn back in its place in the corner by the fire. Mother grumbled about not having any butter today while she slapped and pounded the bread dough on the heavy kitchen table.

"Can we go now?" Barley asked.

"Be home for supper," Mother said. "Though there won't be any butter for your bread, will there? Shoes in the butter churn! What next?"

Barley's shoes made a wet squish, squish, squish all the way to Soldier Jack's place. Rye thought about apologizing, but he was still mad that everyone thought Barley was a great hero while everything Rye did lately seemed to turn out wrong. The boys walked in silence with Barley's squishing shoes doing all the talking.

As they came near Soldier Jack's place, they could hear him squawking out odd sounds on his fiddle. His cow stood lazily in the front yard, chewing her cud and flicking her ears at the most sour notes. Barley and Rye went around the house to where Soldier Jack sat on a stump under a tree with his fiddle tucked under his chin. He had a patch over one eye that only covered part of the long scar that ran from his forehead to his ear. When he saw the boys, he grinned and called out, "Good morning!"

"Good morning, Soldier Jack," Barley said.

"You know boys, I used to know another song, but I've forgotten how it goes." Soldier Jack scratched his thin beard. He hummed a few hesitant notes, then rubbed his fiddle bow across the strings a few more times. He sighed and shook his head.

In the front yard the cow let out a low, "Mooooo."

"So what brings the two of you here on this fine morning?" Soldier Jack leaned the fiddle against the tree trunk behind him.

"We were wondering if you could teach us how to fight with a sword," Rye said.

"How to fight with a sword? It sounds like young Barley here doesn't need any sword fighting lessons. He chased off a whole band of brigands, single-handedly!" Soldier Jack thumped Barley hard on the shoulder.

Rye scuffed his toe in the bare dirt under the tree.

"Well, that's the thing," Barley shot a scowl at Rye. "Some people are saying that I'm not a real fighter, or hero, because I used a magic sword to fight those brigands. I don't really know how to use a real sword."

"I see," Soldier Jack said. "You've certainly come to the right man, that you have. I used to fight in the king's army, that I did. That's where I got this!" he traced his finger from the center of his forehead all along the white puckered line of his scar to his ear. "It's not all fun and games, being a fighter, I'll tell you that!"

"We want to learn, if you'll teach us," Rye said.

"Have you got your own swords?" Soldier Jack asked, narrowing his one good eye.

Barley and Rye raised their wooden swords in the air, the same ones they'd used to pretend to be adventurers before the battle of Lost Castle.

Soldier Jack laughed. "Very well, very well, boys. You want to learn sword fighting, do you? Then I think we can come to some kind of agreement."

END of Episode Four

Episode Five: A Royal Invitation

ONE

As the days went by, life in Humble Village returned to normal. Since there were no more brigands to fear, the children were allowed to cross the bridge and go over the river so long as they didn't wander into Grayfallow Swamp. Everyone seemed happier and more at ease now that the Lord of Lost Castle was no longer lurking in Lost Forest.

It still rankled Rye whenever someone called Barley a hero, or told Barley what a brave boy he was, but Rye kept that to himself. Someday, Rye thought, he'd get a chance to prove himself. Then everyone in the village would be proud of him too. Especially now that he was a swordsman in training.

Two

Every day when they finished their chores at home, Barley and Rye ran down the road to Soldier Jack's place at the other end of the village. Once they were there, Soldier Jack would set them to work chopping wood, mending the fence, or weeding the garden. As the boys worked, Soldier Jack contemplated their sword fighting lesson for the day. Contemplating took a lot of quiet meditation, which Soldier Jack usually did in the shade under the big tree in front of his house, lying on his back with his eyes closed.

When their task for the day was done, Barley and Rye would listen attentively as Soldier Jack shared his deep and expansive knowledge of swordsmanship.

"There's four main things you've got to know," Soldier Jack said one afternoon, the same as he did at every lesson. "The first is the advance. You do that by stepping forward. Now let's see you do it. Advance."

Barley and Rye advanced.

"Good, now do it some more."

The two boys advanced all the way to the end of Soldier Jack's yard and then back, one step at a time.

"Good, very good. Now the next thing you need is the retreat. You do that by stepping backward."

"But why would we want to retreat?" Barley asked. "I thought retreating was for cowards."

"If you never took on a fight unless you were certain you could win it, what kind of a hero would you be? Tell me that!" Soldier Jack said. "If you find you've taken on more than you can handle, that's when you want to retreat. No shame in that. Besides, then you can live to fight another day!"

Barley and Rye retreated, walking backward, all the way to the far end of the yard. Soldier Jack followed them, nodding his head wisely.

"Now for the attack," Soldier Jack said. "Stick out your sword arm, like this." He thrust his arm forward, an imaginary sword in his grip.

Barley and Rye each thrust their wooden swords out in front of them.

"Do it again. Do it a hundred times. You count, I'll meditate," Soldier Jack said.

Barley and Rye counted to a hundred as they practiced their attack. Rye had to thump Soldier Jack on the shoulder to rouse him from his meditation when they were ready for the next part of the lesson.

"Now last of all, the parry." Soldier Jack yawned. "This is where you knock your enemy's sword out of the way so he doesn't hit you."

"Yes, you've told us," Rye said. "Every day since our first lesson."

Soldier Jack didn't seem to hear. "Now Barley, you attack, and Rye, you parry. A hundred times. Do it."

"Are you sure this is all there is to it?" Barley asked as Rye whacked away Barley's forty-seventh attack.

"Huh?" Soldier Jack said. He seemed to be meditating again.

"Isn't there anything more you're going to teach us?" Barley asked.

"This is all there is. From here on out, it's a matter of practice, practice, practice. And knowing when to do which one."

"Yes, how do we know when to do which one?" Rye asked, smashing Barley's sixty-fourth attack.

"Practice first. We'll get to that later."

THREE

So Barley and Rye practiced. Rye would attack and advance while Barley would parry and retreat. Then they would switch. On occasion, when he wasn't meditating too deeply, Soldier Jack would shout advice like, "Hold your arm higher, Rye," or "Keep your sword more in line when you parry, Barley," or, "You're not chopping wood, are you? It's a sword, not a hatchet!"

When Soldier Jack fell to meditating very deeply, Barley and Rye forgot about practicing and simply fought. Barley's bold attacks made their mark a lot more than Rye would like to admit, and Rye's clever feints didn't always fool Barley the way he hoped. Still, Rye thought he was just a little bit better than Barley at sword fighting. Just a little bit. One of his favorite tricks was to retreat until Barley thought he had Rye on the run. Then Rye would make a sudden attack that his overconfident brother wasn't prepared for. It worked most of the time.

Every evening, Barley and Rye dragged themselves home after practice, rubbing their bruises and complaining about their aching muscles. Mother would shake her head and click her tongue to see their scraped knuckles and the purple welts on their arms and legs. But no matter what, the next day after chores were done, the boys rushed to Soldier Jack's place for more.

One afternoon, in the middle of Rye cleverly dodging a ferocious attack from Barley, a sudden strange sound came from the direction of the village. Both boys stopped fighting to listen. It started out like a cow's moo, but then jumped up high and fluttered around like geese honking, and then settled into a long bleat like a goat.

Soldier Jack jumped up. "By my beard, I haven't heard that in a long time!"

"What is it?" Barley asked. "I've never heard it at all."

"It's the royal summons. It means a messenger has come from the king himself to Humble Village! Come along, boys, let's go see what the king has to say."

Four

Barley and Rye ran to the village green where everyone had gathered around a tall man on horseback. The man had large front teeth and not much of a chin. He wore a red velvet cap with a fluffy black feather, a red and black striped velvet jacket, black trousers and red boots. His legs were so long that the stirrups hung down well below his horse's knees. In his hand he held a long, shiny, golden trumpet. He put it to his lips and puffed his cheeks until his face was as red as his hat, then blew the same sounds that Barley and Rye had heard when they were in Soldier Jack's yard.

By then, everyone in the village was gathering on the green. Excited whispers flew through the growing crowd. Barley and Rye had never seen a royal messenger in their village before. Their mother and father came to join them as the messenger blew on his trumpet a third time.

After the third trumpet call, the messenger tucked his trumpet under one arm and whipped out a long roll of parchment. "Hear ye, villagers of Humble Village. His Royal Majesty, King Hugric, wishes to congratulate the mighty hero who has driven the Lord of Lost Castle from his stronghold and banished him from the Lost Forest."

Barley grinned from ear to ear. Rye threw back his head and moaned.

"For this noble deed, the king renders his thanks, and hereby declares that he who has done this deed is to come to the king's castle at once to be made a knight of the realm." The messenger looked up from his parchment. "I will be escorting him there myself." He glanced haughtily around at the crowd.

Many of the villagers cheered and clapped. Some of them looked confused. Barley turned pink as a pickled beet. Rye's mother gasped in delight and hugged Rye's father, who stared at the messenger in disbelief. Rye rubbed at his ears, wondering if he'd heard correctly. Barley was going to be made a knight? This was so infinitely unfair.

"Would the brave warrior who defeated the Lord of Lost Castle please come forward?"

In a happy daze, Barley walked toward the messenger. The other villagers stepped back to make room for him.

FIVE

"I said," the messenger shouted, "would the brave warrior who defeated the Lord of Lost Castle please come forward. We have heard that he is a resident of this village. The king wishes to bestow upon him the highest honor in the land!"

Barley stood so close to the messenger's horse he could almost reach out and touch it.

"If he is not here, then..." the messenger seemed to notice Barley for the first time. "You there, little boy, stand back please. I am looking for the warrior who defeated the Lord of Lost Castle. Do you know where he is?"

"Yes," Barley said. "It's me. I defeated the Lord of Lost Castle."

"Ha ha, very funny. Now go run and fetch him for me, if he's even here in this village. I am beginning to have my doubts." The messenger frowned suspiciously at the crowd. Rye noticed for the first time how shabby and plain all the villagers' clothes were compared to the messenger's colorful suit.

"But it was Barley who defeated the Lord of Lost Castle," Tildy Weaver said. "I was there! I saw it."

"Yes, it was our Barley," said another villager.

"He's standing right in front of you," said a third. "Can you not see?"

"Do you mean to say this child defeated the Lord of Lost Castle?" The messenger's face grew redder than when he'd been blowing his trumpet. "What do you take me for? Is this some kind of joke? I'll have you know I am an official messenger of His Majesty, King Hugric, and I will not be trifled with!"

"He had a magic sword from the witch," Rye shouted out over the crowd. "That's how he did it."

"A magic sword?" the messenger seemed interested. "May I see this magic sword? Is it the one you're carrying?"

"No." Barley hid his battered wooden sword behind his back. "I gave the magic sword back to the Witch of Lost Castle."

"Ah, then." The messenger coughed a few times and fiddled with his trumpet. "Well, then. You mean to say that this child is truly the one who defeated the Lord of Lost Castle?"

"Yes!" everyone in the village chorused.

"He didn't have any help from anyone? Anyone older, or more warrior-like?" the messenger asked.

"I had to go by myself," Barley said. "The witch didn't even come to the castle with me."

"Well, then," the messenger said. He glanced at the scroll in his hand and then rolled it up. "I am afraid I must be going now. Good day." The messenger gave his horse a kick and it started to trot off through the crowd.

SIX

"Wait a moment now!" Barley's mother ran up and grabbed the bridle of the messenger's horse. "You said the hero who defeated the Lord of Lost Castle was to be made a knight, by order of the king! You're to escort him, you said. We all heard you. How can you do that if you leave now? My Barley needs time to pack his things for a long journey like that."

"My good woman, I have no intention of taking this child to the king to be knighted. No one would believe that he was the one who defeated the Lord of Lost Castle. I would be a laughingstock. I would probably lose my position. And so I shall simply tell the king I was unable to find the man he is looking for."

An angry murmur ran through the crowd. Mother held the bridle tight.

"Kindly unhand my horse and let me pass!" the messenger said. "Do you know the penalty for obstructing a messenger of the king?"

Barley planted himself square in front of the messenger's horse. "You're a coward," Barley said.

"I beg your pardon!" The messenger gritted his teeth.

"You're going to disobey your king, simply because you're afraid of the truth," Barley said.

"Out of my way, peasant!" The messenger's voice grew high and shrill. He glared angrily at Barley.

"I'm not afraid of you," Barley said. "I saw that same look in the eyes of the Lord of Lost Castle. I didn't retreat. I kept fighting until I saw that look turn to fear. I didn't retreat then, and I'm not going to retreat now."

The messenger stared at Barley. The anger on his face turned to surprise. Rye stared too. He'd never heard his brother talk this way before. Maybe there had been a little something more to Barley than being lucky enough to get his hands on a magic sword.

No one in the crowd moved or dared to speak.

"I do believe you are the one who defeated the Lord of Lost Castle," the messenger said at last. "Very well, I will take you to the king and let him decide what to do with you."

SEVEN

The crowd cheered and clapped, all except Rye. He wrapped his arms around his middle and gave Barley a sad, longing look. Rye imagined Barley going off to the king's castle and becoming a knight and having adventures while he himself stayed in the village and milked cows the rest of his life.

Barley turned his grinning face to Rye. When he saw his brother, his expression changed.

"Wait," Barley shouted over the crowd.

The crowd quieted.

"One more thing. My brother must come with me," Barley said.

This surprised Rye even more than when Barley had stood up to the messenger.

"Aye, he must!" Rye's father said. He clapped a hand on Rye's shoulder. "Barley is too young to travel alone, and his mother and I must stay here and tend to the farm. Rye must go too."

The messenger looked stern for a moment and Rye was afraid he'd say no. Then the messenger laughed. "I suppose the two of you put together just about make up one grown-up person. I'll take you both to the king. Be ready to leave in half an hour. I want to make it to the next village by sundown."

"Hooray!" shouted Barley. He ran for their cottage with Rye at his heels.

EIGHT

As they ran, Rye kept trying to think of something to say to
Barley. He was grateful that Barley had wanted him to go
along, but he couldn't get over the fact that Barley was going
to be made a knight. What would that mean? Would Rye
have to call him Sir Barley? Would Barley get a nice sword,
and a horse, and armor? It had been bad enough when the
villagers brought Barley presents to thank him for rescuing
their children from Lost Castle. Rye wasn't sure how he felt
about Barley getting to have so many things Rye had always
dreamed of.

For a tiny instant, Rye thought he might refuse to go. He
would stay right here in Humble Village. Barley could go see
the king all by himself, and then go off on his knightly
adventures, and never come home ever again, for all Rye
cared.

But then Rye thought about how he had always wanted
to go and see the king's castle, and King's Town. If he went
along with Barley, he would probably get to see the king
himself. He couldn't miss out on that.

Besides, maybe, just maybe, Barley might need him.

The two boys reached the house, all out of breath. They
ran in and climbed the ladder to the loft. Barley threw two
pairs of socks and his pillow into the middle of his blanket,

then rolled it up and tied it with string. "Ready!" he announced, hefting his bundle onto his shoulder.

Rye found his own spare socks and added a scarf, a tinderbox, a few candles, his best knife, and a tin cup. He rolled up his blanket and tied it.

Barley surprised him by tackling him with a hug. "Thanks for coming with me," Barley said. He let go of Rye and sat down on his bed with a plop. "I'm scared, Rye. I don't know anything about being a knight."

"I don't suppose there's much to it," Rye said. He poked a finger through the ragged hole in his wide-brimmed farmer's hat and then tugged it onto his head. "You just ride around in fancy armor and slay dragons and such."

Barley's blue eyes stared, wide and frightened.

"Oh yes," Rye said. "Large dragons, fire-breathing, teeth and claws. It's what's knights do."

Barley hugged his blanket roll tight.

"Of course if you don't want to be a knight, you can just say the word and I'm sure the messenger will let us stay." Rye suggested.

"No," Barley jumped up. "I'm going."

NINE

"Barley! Rye!" Father's voice called as he stepped in through the front door.

"We're here!" Barley shouted back.

"Do you have everything you need?" Mother's voice came up from below.

"All set," Rye said.

"This is so exciting!" Mother said as Barley and Rye climbed down the ladder. "Do you know what this means? Barley will have a title and land of his own, maybe even his own castle. The king is a generous and good man. I hope you won't have to live too far away, Barley dear. Or maybe we can all come live in your castle with you!"

"Now, Mother," Father said, "let's not get ahead of ourselves. The king's not expecting a little peasant boy, as the messenger said."

Mother took Barley by the shoulders. "Listen. The king said you were to be made a knight. A good king never goes back on his word. Don't you let him go back on his word."

"No, Mama, I won't," Barley said.

"I can't believe you're leaving us again." Mother went to the kitchen. She sniffled and wiped her eyes with the corner of her apron. "It seems you've only just come home."

"You should take old Lumpy," Father said. "You'll need to ride to keep up with the messenger. If you're not back in time for harvesting, I'll borrow an ox from the Grovers."

"Thank you, Father," Rye said. He hadn't even thought about needing a horse and he certainly hoped they'd be home in time for the harvest. It wasn't that far to King's Town, was it?

"I'll go and get him ready," Father ducked out the door.

Mother packed two bags heavy with food. She gave one to each of them, then wrapped her sons in a big hug.

From outside on the road came an impatient bleat from the messenger's trumpet.

"Hurry away now, boys! Come back to us soon. We'll be waiting for you." Mother gave them each a kiss.

Barley and Rye ran out the door to find Father standing by the road, holding Lumpy by the bridle. The king's messenger had a pout on his face as he looked over Lumpy's knobbly knees and splotchy grey coat.

Father helped Barley up, then held Lumpy steady while Rye climbed up behind. Mother came running out with Barley's hat and handed it up to him.

"Are you ready?" the messenger asked.

"Ready!" Barley turned to grin at Rye.

The messenger gave his horse a kick, Rye clicked his tongue at Lumpy, and they started off. Rye looked back to see his parents waving to them from the front gate. "Goodbye Mother! Goodbye Father!" he called.

"Bring that rascal Barley back to us!" Father shouted.

"I will!" Rye said, though he thought it was his job to be the family rascal. Barley had always been good as gold. Rye wasn't sure he could be the responsible one for a change, but he would try. "I promise!"

END of Episode Five

EPISODE SIX: A KNIGHT'S ERRAND

ONE

Barley and Rye had never been to the next village down the road from their own. They knew it was called Oakbridge Crossing, and that Tildy and Jep Weaver had cousins that lived there, but even though it was only half a day's ride away they had never gone. They never had a reason to.

Near sunset they came around a bend in the river and saw the biggest huddle of houses they'd ever set eyes on. It nestled in a little crook of land between the White River and a swift stream that came tumbling down from the Red Mountains to the west. A sturdy wooden bridge wide enough for a large wagon spanned the stream. The messenger's horse crossed the bridge with a prim clip-clip-clip while Barley and Rye's horse clop-clopped behind.

Barley and Rye stared in wonder at the neat rows of houses. Their village only had one row of houses strung out along the main road, but this village had a spider's web of streets stretching between the river and the stream, with more houses spilling into the countryside.

"We could stay with Jep and Tildy's cousins if we can find them," Rye suggested. The messenger didn't seem to hear, or care. He rode straight on until they came to the center of town, where a simple stone fountain poured water into a wide basin. Villagers with buckets and water jars stopped to stare at the king's messenger. They gave puzzled, unwelcoming frowns to the old farm horse with two peasant boys straddling its back.

Without stopping, the messenger rode up to the gate of the largest house in sight. He climbed down from his horse, tied its bridle to the gatepost, then went to the front door and knocked sharply.

"Maybe he knows the people who live here," Barley said.

Rye nodded. It was a big, comfortable-looking house, and from the smell of it they were cooking something good for supper inside.

A girl in a black dress with a white cap and apron opened the door. Light from inside cast a warm yellow glow over the front step. From the surprised look on her face, it was plain she had never seen the messenger before in her life.

"I am a royal messenger on an official errand for the king." The messenger waved a scroll tied with a scarlet ribbon in the girl's face. "I demand lodging for the night."

The girl blinked a few times, then finally seemed to comprehend what the messenger had said. "Oh!" She wrung her hands and curtsied. "Yes, yes, of course. A royal messenger! What an honor, sir. Do come in. And is that your horse? I'll have it put up in the master's stables and properly taken care of, and..." She frowned when she saw Barley and Rye watching from the back of old Lumpy. "You boys be off now! Don't be staring at His Honor the Royal Messenger. He's not a traveling circus show, now, is he? Off you go." She waved them away.

"But we're with him," Barley said.

The girl blinked. Then she laughed. "Sorry, begging your pardon, sir." She gasped for breath then pulled her cap off her head and laughed into it some more. "The imps, the rascals. What a whopper." At last she calmed down to a silly grin and stuffed her hat back on her head. Then she noticed the messenger's face. Her grin disappeared. "Wait, they're not really with you, are they?"

For a long time, the messenger didn't answer. Somewhere in the town, a dog barked. Rye thought maybe the messenger had changed his mind and wasn't going to take them to the king after all. He began making plans to find the Weaver's cousins then ride home in the morning. He hoped Barley wouldn't be too disappointed.

"Yes, they are with me," the messenger said coldly.

The girl let out one sudden, surprised laugh then clapped her hands over her mouth. "Sorry," she said. She narrowed her eyes. "You're demanding lodging for them too, then?"

"We're not demanding anything," Rye said. "We'll gladly work for it. We'll help with the chores, or whatever you need," Rye glanced around the darkening yard, wondering what kind of chores had to be done in such a grand house as this. He didn't see a cow to milk anywhere, or chickens that might need to be fed.

"What, are they in some kind of trouble?" the girl asked the messenger.

"Kindly show me to my room," the messenger said.

"You sharing with the boys, or do you want a room to yourself?" the girl asked, trying very hard not to laugh again.

"A private chamber to myself would be preferable if you have the accommodations," the messenger said.

"Who's that at the door, Hilda?" a man's voice called from inside the house.

"It's the king's royal messenger and a couple of," she paused, as if not sure how to describe Barley and Rye, "young gentlemen he's got in tow. Apparently they're all staying the night, if it pleases you, Master Tropp."

"Well, bring them in and shut the door!" the voice called. "You're letting the night air in."

"You two just leave your horse tied to the post. I'll send Toby to fetch him," the girl said. "Hurry up now. The master wants me to shut the door."

TWO

Barley and Rye scrambled down from Lumpy's back. Rye looped the bridle around the post and followed Barley up the little path to the front door. The door stood tall and wide and round on top, tall enough that not even the messenger had to stoop to go through it. Inside was a little room that didn't seem to be for anything except for walking into the house. Candles flickered from stands hung on the walls. There were stairs to the left, double doors straight ahead, and a small table with a bowl full of flowers on it to the right.

The girl curtsied to the messenger. "This way, sir, up the stairs. There's a nice guest room that should be all ready. I'll have Toby bring up your bags." Then she turned to Barley and Rye. "Wait here and don't touch anything," the girl said, and pointed a sharp finger in their direction. "Don't move, don't breathe, don't nothing!"

"Don't nothing," Rye said to Barley after the girl and the messenger had gone. "That means we ought to do something, right?"

"Now, how did a couple of common sparrows like yourselves come to be traveling with such a fine cock-rooster as that one?" boomed a voice. Barley and Rye jumped. From the top of the stairs a large, bald man in a fine blue velvet jacket frowned down at them. The gold chain around his neck gleamed in the candlelight.

"He's taking us to see the king," Barley said cheerfully. "I'm to be made a knight."

"I don't think he's going to believe that," Rye whispered in alarm. Barley shrugged.

"What was that? I'm not sure I heard correctly." The man came down the stairs, thumping his sturdy cane on each step. "What's your name, boy?" he pointed a finger with a jeweled ring on it at Barley's chest.

"Barley," Barley said. "Barley Fields of Humble Village."

"And how, pray tell, did you come to be in my house?" the man demanded.

"That girl in the black dress let us in, if you please, sir," Barley said.

"If you'd rather us not, we can sleep in the stable," Rye said. "We don't mean to trouble you."

"I'm afraid you don't understand. I meant in the more general sense. What is your story, boy?" the man asked.

"The messenger is taking us to see the king because I defeated the Lord of Lost Castle," Barley said.

"You?" the man said. "You defeated the Lord of Lost Castle?"

"Yes," Barley said.

"Is this true?" The man turned to Rye. "And who are you?"

"I'm his brother. Rye Fields."

"I wonder, did your parents do that on purpose?" The man looked from one boy to the other, his face stern. "No matter. Is what your brother says the truth? Did he defeat the Lord of Lost Castle?"

Rye almost wanted to say of course not, it was just a joke, but he didn't. This wasn't a time to retreat. If Barley had been brave enough to stand up to the messenger, Rye could tell the truth even if this rich man was sure to think it was a lie. "Yes," Rye said. "He did, sir, begging your pardon. I was there."

"Ha ha!" the man laughed. At first Rye thought his laughter meant he didn't believe him, but then the man thumped Barley hard on the back. "So the story is true! It really was a boy from Humble Village who rid us of the brigands. Did you know, boy, that before you ran the Lord of Lost Castle out, I couldn't send my merchant trains through the Lost Forest? They had to go the long way around, or I'd get robbed. Now that the forest is safe, we make the trip through the forest to the Rose Grove Kingdom twice a month. I was rich before, but I'm twice as rich now, and it's all thanks to you! Hilda! Hilda my girl, can you please make up the best room for our young guests here?"

Hilda appeared at the top of the stairs. "I've just given the best room to the royal messenger."

"Then the boys shall have my room and I'll sleep in the stable!"

Rye thought the man must be joking. Surely there were more than enough rooms in the house so that he would never have to sleep in the stable.

"No need for that, sir," the girl said with a giggle. "There's plenty of guest rooms. I'll make them up the second best."

"Make it up for me. I insist these boys should have my room tonight, and tomorrow before they go, I'll see that they're dressed fit to have an audience with the king. See if I won't!"

THREE

That night, Barley and Rye slept in a bed that was larger than the entire loft in their cottage back at home in Humble Village. After a wonderful supper, Hilda had given them each a long linen nightshirt to change into, then whisked away their travel-dusty farm clothes. It took them a while to settle down for sleep because Barley wouldn't stop opening and closing the bed curtains on their jingly metal rings. Rye finally put a stop to it by beating Barley in a pillow fight that left goose feathers everywhere.

In the morning a tailor came and had Barley and Rye try on new jackets and shirts and trousers. The tailor measured and marked then sat down to work while Hilda led the boys, dressed in their freshly-washed farm clothes, down to breakfast.

The messenger was there at the table along with the merchant.

"Ah, here they are!" the merchant said. "I do hope you slept well, boys."

"Yes, we did, thank you," said Rye.

"Sit down and help yourselves," The merchant said.

Barley and Rye sat down and loaded their plates with rolls and slices of ham. As Barley slathered butter on his roll he asked Hilda, who stood by the table, "Have you already eaten?"

BARLEY AND RYE | 113

"No, I'll have mine after I clear up," Hilda said.

"Why don't you join us?" Barley asked.

"Because I'm only the serving girl. I don't sit at table with the master and his guests."

"Oh!" Barley said. "You're a servant? I thought you were his daughter."

Hilda giggled and hid her face behind her cap.

The merchant chuckled too. "So tell us the whole story, Barley Fields. How did you defeat the Lord of Lost Castle?" he asked.

Even the king's messenger watched with interest as Barley told the tale. Rye noticed that the number of brigands in Lost Castle had gone from twenty to fifty since Barley first told the story, and the Lord of Lost Castle himself was now seven feet tall and strong as a troll. Before the story was over, Rye noticed a small crowd of people watching from the hall, all listening. When at last Barley told how he freed the children from a dungeon that was at least a mile underground, everyone cheered and clapped.

Rye still felt jealous, but he had to admit he was proud of Barley too.

By mid-morning the tailor presented each boy with a perfectly fitted suit of fine clothes. They were matching blue, with gold buttons on the jackets. Hilda took them to the cobbler's shop where they each got a good pair of riding boots. On their return to the merchant's house they found Lumpy waiting out front for them, looking very respectable in a blue blanket and new saddle. The merchant's servant handed the reins to Rye while Barley inspected the saddlebags.

"There's a nice picnic lunch in there for you lads," the servant said. "The master would have invited you in, but your king's messenger is in a hurry to be on his way."

The king's messenger, already astride his horse, waited for them while they mounted.

"Now you look presentable!" the merchant said as he came to the door and inspected Barley and Rye.

"Thank you," Barley said with a big grin.

"Yes, thank you, and thanks for everything!" Rye agreed.

"No trouble at all!" the merchant said. "It's the very least I could do. A good journey to you. Come and visit me again any time!"

The merchant and his servants waved goodbye as the messenger led Barley and Rye away.

FOUR

People still stared as Barley and Rye passed through the
town, but these were stares of interest and admiration. Rye
wondered if word had got around about who Barley was
and what he had done. Barley waved at everyone they saw,
and most of them waved back.

That night they came to an even bigger town, one that
was big enough to have its own inn. Barley and Rye got a
room to themselves, and Lumpy got his own stall in the
stable. The next day they rode all day, passing farms and
villages as they travelled up the White River valley, with the
Red Mountains on their left and the Lost Forest on their
right.

One day turned into the next. Each day the towns
seemed larger and the river grew wide and deep enough that
there were often boats sailing along beside them. At last, on
the fifth day, they could see King's Town in the distance,
high on a steep hillside that overlooked the river.

"No boats today," Barley remarked as he stared at the
sparkling water.

"There have been no boats around King's Town for
many a day," the messenger said. "A dragon has come up
from the deep of the sea. Any boat that ventures on the river
will be crushed in its coils."

When the messenger said the word "dragon," Barley stiffened up and gripped the saddle horn in front of him. He watched the water carefully as they rode, but no dragons broke the surface. They did see the wreckage of crushed ships floating against the shore and noticed how no one, not even the birds, would go near the river.

As they got closer to the city, they met more and more people until the road was crowded thick with them. People on horses, people in carts, people on foot, people leading cows, people driving geese, all shouting and bumping and trying to get to the city gate.

The messenger blew his trumpet then cried out, "Make way for the royal messenger and King Hugric's honored guests!"

Slowly, like a frozen stream melting under spring rain, the crowd parted to one side or the other. Everyone stared as Barley and Rye rode up the middle of the road. Barley smiled and waved as if it was all for him, and Rye had to admit that it probably was. A few people waved back. Before long, they were clapping and cheering too. From the way everyone acted, Rye wondered if maybe the whole city had been expecting them.

When they passed through the gatehouse, four mounted soldiers fell in behind them. Their helmets and spear points sparkled in the sun. Now it wasn't just the people in the street who were watching. Windows and doors opened up in all the buildings they passed, and the side streets crowded with people standing on tiptoes to get a look.

They went by a street corner where a small band played on the porch of an inn. As they passed by, the band jumped up to follow. People danced along behind. The cheers and clapping grew louder, and now people were throwing flowers from the upstairs windows. So many people happy to see them! Rye was so dazzled by it all he almost forgot to be jealous.

The parade continued, growing larger and louder, all the way up the hill and to the castle gate. As they came close, the gate swung open only wide enough to let a single horse walk through. The soldiers behind Barley and Rye stopped to hold back the surging crowd. Lumpy obediently followed the messenger's horse through the gate, which thumped closed behind them in a very solid and final sort of way.

"Yay! Hello! Hooray!" Barley's voice slowly faded to an uncertain echo in the vast stone courtyard.

FIVE

Men in red and black uniforms, a little like the messenger's but not as fancy, came and took the horses by the reins. They helped Barley and Rye to the ground.

"Follow me, gentlemen, and I will take you to see King Hugric," the messenger said.

"Wish us luck, Lumpy," Rye whispered, giving the horse a pat.

"And thank you for the ride," said Barley. He gave Lumpy's nose a kiss. "See you soon."

As they walked the long stone hallway, Barley kept reaching for Rye's hand then pulling back. He finally grabbed his own hand and gripped it tight. Rye felt as if he was floating rather than walking. They were about to see the king himself.

At the end of the long hallway stood a tall double door with a guard standing on either side. Two carved eagles with spread wings stared fiercely from the door panels. The messenger stopped in front of the door and straightened his jacket. He nodded to the guards. Rye held his breath as the door swung open.

Pillars tall as trees held up a ceiling high as the sky. Rye's boots clicked on a polished stone floor. Finely dressed lords and ladies stood along the walls, watching curiously as the messenger strode down the long throne room to the raised platform at the far end. There, on a golden throne, topped with a golden eagle stretching its wings, sat King Hugric.

"Your Majesty, if I may be permitted to present Barley Fields of Humble Village, and his brother Rye Fields, also of Humble Village," the messenger said with a bow.

Barley and Rye bowed too.

"Rise," said King Hugric, sounding puzzled. "Did I not command you to bring me the man who single-handedly defeated the Lord of Lost Castle? Where is he?"

"Before you, sire. This boy, Barley Fields, is the person you seek. His whole village avows that it was him, and him alone, who did this great deed."

Gasps and murmurs ran through the crowd, but they weren't excited or even happy. One lady in a billowy yellow gown sobbed into her handkerchief, and a tall man beside her shook his head sadly.

King Hugric himself sat back on his throne, his shoulders sagging. His voice shook a little as he said, "Thank you, my messenger, for your services. Your next task will be to conduct these children home. I believe the customary reward for brave deeds is a bag of gold. Please stop by the treasury and see that this young man is presented with one before you depart. Dismissed."

Rye looked at Barley, who was staring at King Hugric in a daze of stunned shock. Wasn't Barley going to say something? Stand up for himself? What about being made a knight of the realm? A bag of gold was nice, of course, but that wasn't what had been promised.

"Come, boys," the messenger said wearily, with a definite air of I-told-you-so. "Allow me to conduct you to your village again."

REBECCA J. CARLSON | 120

This wasn't time to retreat. Barley's chance at becoming a knight was under attack. It was time to parry. "Wait, didn't the king say that the one who had defeated the Lord of Lost Castle was to be made a knight?" Rye asked. "Isn't that what he said? Is it true? Did he say it?"

The room fell silent.

SIX

"You are not to speak in the presence of the king without permission. Did I not tell you this?" the messenger said fiercely. He grabbed Rye by the elbow and Barley by the collar and began towing them toward the double doors at the back of the room.

"My mother says we have a good king, and a good king never goes back on his word," Rye called out.

"Messenger, hold," King Hugric said.

The messenger stopped, huffed, and dragged the boys around to face the king. He glared angrily at Rye.

"My good subject," King Hugric said to Rye. "I am sure you and your brother imagine knighthood to be a great honor that brings wealth and fame to the bearer of it. All this is true, but it also carries a great responsibility. I will tell you why I wished to knight the man who was strong enough to defeat the Lord of Lost Castle. It is because a knight's sworn duty is to protect the realm, and our realm is in grave danger. We need a great warrior, a hero, who can fight to protect us. If I make your brother a knight, I will be sending an innocent child to his death. Now, tell me, Rye Fields of Humble Village, what do you think a good king should do?"

Rye hung his head. He didn't want Barley in any danger. King Hugric was right. Rye felt foolish for thinking that his brother might actually be made a knight of the realm. It was impossible, just as the messenger had said. Time to retreat.

"What's the danger?" Barley asked. "What would I have to do?"

Rye looked up in surprise, then shook his head at Barley. They'd best take their bag of gold, go home, and not trouble the king any further.

"Oh, my child," King Hugric said sadly. "You would be required to slay the dragon of the deep."

Barley froze, his blue eyes wide with terror.

"Sorry to trouble you, Sire," the messenger said. "With your permission, we'll take our leave now."

"I'll do it," Barley said, his voice loud but trembling. "I'll borrow the magic sword again from the Witch of Lost Castle. She said I could, if I ever needed it."

"Twelve knights have already been slain by this dragon, and we are beginning to lose hope of ever defeating it," King Hugric said. "I cannot ask you to do this thing."

"It's a good sword," Barley said. "No enemy can stand against it. That's the magic of it."

King Hugric thought for a moment. "And is this how you defeated the Lord of Lost Castle? With a magic sword?"

"Yes," said Barley, "Though I've been learning to use a regular sword too, haven't I, Rye?"

"You don't have to do this, Barley," Rye said. "We should go home."

"Then perhaps this is the service I should require of you," King Hugric said. "Bring the magic sword, and we will find a man who can wield it against the dragon. Bring the sword, and I will keep my word and make you a knight."

"Yes, your majesty," Barley said with a bow.

END of Episode Six

Episode Seven: The Thirteenth Knight

ONE

The king granted Barley and Rye each a fine horse to ride, food, and supplies for the journey, and even appointed a knight to be their escort. Barley and Rye said good-bye to Lumpy, who was taking a long and well-earned rest in a private stall in the royal stables, and set out to seek Lost Castle.

"I'm terribly glad you two showed up when you did," the knight, whose name was Sir Pinsky, said on the third evening of their journey as they camped on the plains between the White River and the Lost Forest. Rye thought that if he didn't know Sir Pinsky was a knight, he would not have guessed it. True, Sir Pinsky had a sword with the crest of the Knights of the Land Far Away engraved on the pommel, which was stashed with the rest of his gear out of sight in his tent, but other than that he was remarkably unremarkable. He wasn't very tall, had straight brown hair, a short moustache, and a plain, friendly face. "I would have been the next knight to face the dragon, you know." He stirred the fire and made a nervous little chuckle. "But now I'll have a magic sword to help me. That should improve my chances immensely."

Barley and Rye gave each other a look.

"I think we'll be off to bed now," Rye said.

"Oh," Sir Pinsky said. "Good night, then."

Alone in their tent, Barley kept his voice down so Sir Pinsky wouldn't hear. "He's not exactly my idea of a brave adventurer."

"Well, the king said that the dragon already ate the twelve bravest knights in the kingdom, so that makes him only the thirteenth bravest," Rye said. "It would make sense that he's a little… disappointing."

"It's not fair he gets to use my sword," Barley said. "With my magic sword, I could slay the dragon just as well as he could."

So could I, Rye thought. *So could I.*

TWO

Early the next morning the travelers reached the edge of the Lost Forest.

"This is about the same place that we came out, don't you think, Rye?" Barley asked.

Rye studied the shape of the Red Mountains rising above the distant river, considered the sunny, grassy plain around them, and then peered into the shadows under the trees. "Yes, this looks like the right place. If we go due east from here, we should find the place where the castle was."

"Sounds simple enough," Sir Pinsky said.

"Not entirely simple," Rye said. "The castle doesn't always stay in the same place."

"Oh," Sir Pinsky said. "How often does it move?"

Rye didn't know.

"Only one way to find out," Sir Pinsky said. "Onward into the forest we go."

They led their horses along a narrow dirt track through the shady forest but found that it quickly turned around and led them out onto the plains again. Sir Pinsky spotted another path between the trees, but it led to a wide bog and they had to turn around and go back out the way they had come. Next, Rye saw a little stream that they followed into the forest until it ended in a spring at the base of a cliff. The cliff was too steep to climb, and the trees were too dense on either side for them to pass.

"I'm beginning to think the forest doesn't want us in here," Rye said.

Sir Pinsky drew his sword. "We'll not be defeated so easily! Never fear! I will cut our way through."

Barley and Rye sat on their horses while Sir Pinsky hacked at a tree with his sword. Bits of wood flew here and there, but the tree didn't seem to be much damaged. As Rye tried to think of a polite way to tell Sir Pinsky to stop, he noticed a squeaking sound, like fast little hiccups. He turned to see a red squirrel perched on a nearby branch.

"Do you see that squirrel?" Rye asked Barley.

"Yes," Barley said.

"I think it's laughing at us," Rye said.

"Hey squirrel!" Barley said. "Are you laughing at us?"

"Yes!" the squirrel squeaked.

Sir Pinsky yelped and dropped his sword. "Did that squirrel speak, or are one of you boys a ventriloquist?"

"It was the squirrel," Rye said in amazement. Perhaps he shouldn't have been so surprised. Barley had told him about the talking deer he'd met in Lost Forest.

Barley said, "What's so funny, squirrel?"

"You'll never get through that way. The forest doesn't want you." The squirrel's ears and tail stiffened up, and he said very seriously, "You'd better go back the way you came before the trees decide to move in all around you. They'll trap you like you're in like a wooden cage and never let you out."

Rye glanced nervously behind them. It did seem like the trees between them and the edge of the forest were thicker than they had been before.

"What way should we go to get to Lost Castle?" Barley asked.

Sir Pinsky warned, "I'm not so sure it's wise to ask directions from a talking squirrel. I think I read something about it in the Valorous Knight's Handbook of Adventuring."

The squirrel stood up on its hind legs and pointed with a small furry paw. "Out! Back the way you came! No need to go stomping around with your big, smelly horses where you're not wanted."

"Please," Rye said, "We're trying to find Lost Castle."

The squirrel laughed so hard he fell out of the tree.

"You can't find Lost Castle!" The squirrel waved its tiny, furry paw in the air. "That's why they call it Lost Castle. It's lost. Go back to where you came from, silly humans!"

Barley said, "But the witch said if I ever needed to borrow the magic sword again, I'd know where to find her."

The squirrel stopped laughing. It sat up eagerly. "Wait a minute. Are you the boy who defeated the Lord of Lost Castle? With the magic sword?"

Rye felt a twinge of jealousy. Even this talking squirrel knew Barley was a hero.

"The very same, at your service," Barley said with a grin.

The squirrel leapt up onto Barley's boot, dashed around him once as he climbed, and ended up on top of Barley's head. Hanging onto Barley's hair, the squirrel dangled himself upside down so that he was nose to nose with Barley.

"Hmmm," the squirrel studied Barley hard. Then he declared. "I believe you."

"Thank you," Barley said. "Now get off my head." He brushed the squirrel away.

The squirrel jumped to the nearest tree branch.

"Can you help us?" Rye asked the squirrel. "Do you know where the castle is?"

"So what if I did?" The squirrel walked along the branch, swishing his tail as if he didn't care much one way or another. "What would be in it for me if I told you?"

"Would you like something to eat?" Barley opened a saddle bag. "I've got a biscuit here, and I think we still have some almonds."

"You wouldn't happen to have a piece of cheese, would you?" the squirrel asked.

"Cheese? Squirrels don't eat cheese," Rye said.

"I adore cheese!" The squirrel melted into a puddle of red fur in a crook of the branch. "Absolutely the best thing I've ever tasted. I hardly ever get it, living here in the forest. I'd do anything for a bit of cheese." He raised his head with a hopeful gleam in his eye.

"I've got some cheese right here." Barley pinched a piece off the wedge of cheese in his saddlebag and held it out to the squirrel.

"Thanks!" the squirrel jumped to Barley's hand, snatched the cheese, and was back on the branch before Rye could blink. Rye watched the squirrel suspiciously.

"Now where's the castle?" Barley said.

The squirrel chewed, and then he swallowed. "No idea," he said.

"You thieving little beastie!" Rye said.

"I said it wasn't wise to have dealings with a talking squirrel," Sir Pinsky said.

"But the birds know," the squirrel said. He licked his whiskers as if hoping to find a small particle of cheese he'd left behind. "They can see it from the air. I'll just go find one and ask. Stay right where you are. I'll be right back."

THREE

Barley, Rye, and Sir Pinsky waited in the forest by the little
spring under the cliff. The trees never moved while they
were looking at them, but Rye felt certain that they were still
somehow closing in. The three of them kept watch, each in a
different direction, in case the trees could somehow move
when no one had their eyes on them.

After a long time, Sir Pinsky said, "We should go back
and try another way into the forest."

"No, wait," Barley said. "I hear something."

Rye listened. It might have been the wind in the trees
somewhere far off, making a faint rustling and whistling.
Then again it might not. The sound came closer and closer,
and suddenly down through the canopy of leaves came a
whole flock of speckled starlings. They perched on the trees
until the branches were black with them.

"Hello, birds!" Barley said. Rye could barely hear him
over all the chirping. "Can you show us the way to Lost
Castle?"

The birds crowded on the closest branches, jostling and
knocking each other off into the air. They eyed the
saddlebags with great interest.

More creatures wanting our food, Rye thought. The squirrel
must have told them to come and get a free meal from the
silly humans.

"Do you want some biscuits?" Barley asked.

The birds didn't say anything, but they got even more excited when Barley pulled a dried biscuit from the saddlebag.

"Wait, Barley," Rye said.

"It won't do any harm," Barley said. "Even if they don't show us the way." He crumbled the biscuit and dropped it to the ground. The birds dove from the tree branches and carpeted the forest floor. The horses shuffled nervously, trying to avoid the squawking, rolling mass of wings and beaks and bright eyes. When every last crumb was gone, the birds all rose into the air.

"Congratulations," Rye said. "You've just fed some of our rations to a bunch of useless birds."

"No, look!" Barley said. "They *are* showing us which way to go!"

The birds swarmed in the air only a short distance away, swirling in a dark cloud, as if waiting for something.

"Maybe they are," Sir Pinsky said. "Let's try following them and see what they do next."

The horses pushed their way through the undergrowth. When they had nearly reached the birds, the flock moved. Barley, Rye, and Sir Pinsky kept following the birds through the forest as best they could. The birds didn't seem to care about leading them across ravines or through thick patches of thorns. Being birds, it didn't make any difference to them what was on the ground. Sometimes the birds had to wait impatiently in the trees while Barley, Rye, and Sir Pinsky figured out how to make their way safely through a bog or over a steep cliff.

"I think these birds are only doing this for sport," Sir Pinsky said as he plucked thorns out of his leather breeches.

"I don't recognize any of this," Rye added, looking at the forest all around them.

"That doesn't mean anything. The castle moves around, remember?" Barley said. "Let's keep going."

The birds led them deeper into the forest all through the afternoon. At last, when he was just about to suggest they find a place to camp for the night, Rye caught sight of a tower rising above the trees.

"Is that it?" he pointed

"Yes!" Barley said, "That's it! We found it."

"Good!" Sir Pinsky said, dumping water out of his boots from the last river the birds had led them across. "I've had enough of being guided by birds."

"Thank you, birds!" Barley said. He crumbled another biscuit for them and left them happily fighting over the crumbs.

The three travelers rode toward the castle gate but stopped when they saw the guards. Seven gray wolves kept watch over Lost Castle. There were three on one side of the open gate, three on the other side, and one directly in front. The horses whinnied and shied away.

Sir Pinsky forced his horse forward. "We seek an audience with the Witch of Lost Castle," he said uncertainly, as if he wasn't sure the wolves would understand him.

The wolves growled in reply. Rye patted his nervous horse and hoped the wolves wouldn't decide to attack them. They were some of the biggest wolves that Rye had ever seen.

"Please," Barley said. "I'm Barley Fields. I defeated the Lord of Lost Castle. The witch said I could borrow the magic sword if I needed it. Please tell her we'd like to see her."

The growls stopped. One wolf cocked his head and narrowed its eyes, as if thinking about what Barley had said.

They started to talk among themselves with soft yips, whines, and twitches of their ears. At last the wolf who had stood right in front of the gate turned and went inside. When Barley urged his horse forward to follow, the other six wolves growled and lined up in front of the gate to block the way.

Barley stayed where he was.

"Perhaps we should leave," Sir Pinsky said after a few minutes.

"Wait," Rye said. "Let's see what happens."

When a few minutes had gone by, the wolf who had gone into the castle returned with a young deer walking at his side. The deer stared at Barley, then nodded his head. The wolf gave a sharp bark, and the other six wolves moved back to their positions at either side of the gate.

"The two boys may come inside," the wolf said in a low, rough voice. "The horses and the man must stay out here."

Barley and Rye dismounted and handed the reins to Sir Pinsky.

Sir Pinsky leaned down and said in a whisper, "If there's any trouble in there, boys, just give a shout and I'll be there in a wink."

Rye doubted that Sir Pinsky would be much help if there was trouble.

"Don't worry about us," Rye said. "We'll be right back."

"Hello," Barley said to the deer. "Are you the one I helped in the swamp?"

"Yes," the deer said in a soft, shy voice. "Hello, Barley."

Barley hugged the deer around the neck. "You're almost as big as me now!" he said in surprise.

The deer bumped his black nose against Barley's face.

"Do you live here in the castle? Where's your mother? How have you been? It's so good to see you!" Barley said. He turned in a circle to watch the deer prance happily around him.

The big wolf chuckled. "Slowly now, he's still learning to speak human."

"Follow me," The deer said, and led them in through the open castle gate.

FOUR

The inside of Lost Castle had changed a lot since Barley and Rye last saw it. Instead of smoke-stained walls covered with sprawling ivy, clean gray stone sheltered the courtyard. A badger pulled weeds in a tidy vegetable garden near the kitchen door and a team of brown rabbits hauled a bucket up from the well. The sight of the large wheel that held the chain to raise and lower the gate sent Rye a rush of bad memories from his time spent imprisoned here, but he pushed them aside.

The deer led them up a stairway and down a short gallery with a doorway guarded by two foxes at the end. The foxes bowed to them politely as they passed. Barley and Rye and entered a room with wooden pillars carved like trees, complete with wooden leaves spreading over the ceiling. A small figure in green robes sat on a wooden throne at the far end of the room.

"Come in!" called a familiar, cracked voice. "I hope you had a pleasant journey."

"It was pleasant enough," Rye said, pulling a last thorn from the bottom edge of his jacket.

"I'm glad to see you. In fact, I'm surprised you stayed away so long," the witch said with a smile. Her teeth were still crooked, and her spindly arms and legs still stuck out from her round little body like she was some kind of spider,

but her ragged black clothes had been changed for fine green
robes. Her crown, instead of being on her head, rested on a
pillow on a carved wooden table beside her throne. She had
a long wooden staff in her hand, decorated with twining ivy
vines. A glossy black raven with a quill pen clutched in one
foot scribbled something in a fat book laid open at the base of
the throne.

"Names, please," The raven cawed.

"Barley Fields, of Humble Village," Barley said.

"Rye Fields, of the same," Rye said with a bow.

"I suppose you've come to borrow the sword?" the witch
said with a knowing smile.

The sword itself hung on the wall behind the witch's
throne. It gleamed softly in the light coming through the
green glass windows.

"Yes," Barley said.

"You don't seem too excited about it," the witch said.

"It isn't for me to use, you see. I'm borrowing it for King
Hugric who will loan it to one of his knights, Sir Pinsky, who
will use it to slay the Dragon of the Deep."

"Hmmmm," the witch stroked the one long hair coming
out of a wart on her chin.

"I promise I'll bring it back when it's all done," Barley
said.

"That's not what's worrying me," the witch said. "You
might have wondered why I chose a child to wield the sword
and take back my castle."

"Yes, why did you?" Rye said, more sharply than he
meant to.

The witch's eyebrows shot up. "It's because a child's
motives are simple. You, young Rye, can only hold one true
intent in your heart at a time. The same goes for your
brother, Barley. A grown-up person, though, has many

intentions in his heart, all working at the same time, some working against the others. I'm afraid Sir Pinky may have a hard time purifying his heart in order to be truly unselfish."

"It's Sir Pinsky," Rye said. He'd always thought Sir Pinsky wouldn't be much use.

"You mean he might not be able to use the sword?" Barley asked.

"A definite possibility," the witch said.

"No matter," Rye said quickly. He turned to Barley. "The king said that all you had to do was bring him the sword, and then he would make you a knight. After we bring the sword, then they can worry about what to do with the dragon."

"I'm going to have to fight the dragon myself, aren't I?" Barley looked pale.

Rye shook his head. "Not if you don't want to. Besides, the other night you said you wanted the chance."

"I didn't say I wanted to. I said I could."

"Enough, boys, enough." The witch held up her hand. "I haven't yet decided if I should loan you the sword for the purpose you have described to me."

"What?" Barley and Rye said in chorus.

"But you said, if I needed it..." Barley pleaded.

"It sounds as if it is King Hugric who needs it, not you. True, King Hugric is my neighbor, and it's a neighborly thing to loan something to a neighbor in need. I do, however, want to be sure I get my something back. As good as your intentions are, Barley, if you put this sword in King Hugric's possession, the decision of what to do with it is no longer yours. You can make me no promises."

"He'll give it back," Barley said. "He's a good king."

"Hmmmm," said the witch again, narrowing her eyes.

"But if you don't loan us the sword, what do we do about the dragon?" Rye asked, "Is there another way to fight it?"

"It's eating all the boats," Barley said. "You should see the river. Nothing can come near it for fear of the dragon. We have to do something."

"I will have to think about this," the witch said. "You two and your knight can stay in the castle tonight and I will tell you my decision in the morning."

FIVE

A great feast was held at Lost Castle in honor of Barley and Rye and Sir Pinsky. Nuts, berries, and heaps of greens covered the table. There were dripping pieces of honeycomb, fresh sweet onions and carrots, platters of roasted fish with mushrooms, and sour little crab apples for dessert. The animals talked and laughed, sometimes in human words and sometimes in their own sounds. The witch said very little, watching the boys and Sir Pinsky thoughtfully as she nibbled on clover and dandelion greens. Rye noticed that Sir Pinsky stared a lot, didn't eat very much, and laughed too loudly at the jokes. He obviously never had dinner in a banquet hall full of talking woodland animals. Barley, on the other hand, seemed perfectly at ease, especially with his friend the deer standing beside him.

As for Rye, he enjoyed himself, but couldn't forget his worry about what would happen tomorrow. Barley seemed determined to do something about the Dragon of the Deep. This was a good thing. Rye agreed that something ought to be done, but he wasn't sure that Barley was the one who ought to do it. He hoped the witch would let Sir Pinsky use the sword. He didn't want Barley in danger. In fact, if Sir Pinsky couldn't use the sword, Rye was not going to let Barley use it either. He wasn't going to let Barley anywhere near that dragon. Rye would fight the dragon himself first.

After the meal, a troupe of field mice performed a tragic play about a lost princess and the raven sang an old song about a unicorn who ran away to sea to become a pirate. Then the animals asked Barley to tell the story of how he defeated the Lord of Lost Castle. Barley happily agreed. Rye noticed he didn't exaggerate so much this time, not with the witch listening.

When the story was over and Barley came to sit back down, Sir Pinsky said quietly, "That sword seems a tricky one to use. It has a lot of rules."

"Only two," Barley said, leaning in front of Rye to talk to Sir Pinsky. "You have to have an unselfish heart, and you've got to be fighting someone who's standing up. It isn't that complicated."

Sir Pinsky didn't reply.

After dinner, Barley's friend the deer showed Barley and Rye to their room. Sir Pinsky was led reluctantly off in another direction. He'd been hanging close to Barley and Rye as if he very much wanted human company in this castle full of animals and gave them a longing look as two foxes led him off down another hallway.

"I'm not sure I want to be a knight anymore," Barley said as the two boys climbed into a pair of tidy feather beds in a room hung with green tapestries. A cheerful little fire burned in the fireplace.

"Why not?" Rye asked, irritated that Barely had come all this way only to figure this out now.

"Sir Pinsky is a knight, but he's really just an ordinary person. I thought becoming a knight would make me braver, or stronger, or better somehow. But maybe it won't."

"It will make you richer," Rye said.

"I don't care about being richer," Barley said. "I want adventures. I've had plenty of adventures already without being a knight. I can have plenty more, all on my own."

"Going on adventures takes money. If you haven't got a lot of money, you have to work if you want to eat. Knights can go about on adventures because they have bags of gold to buy everything they need. We can't go on adventures because we're farmers."

"We're on an adventure right now," Barley said.

"One with a dragon at the end of it," Rye said.

"That's another reason I don't think I want to be a knight," Barley said in a small voice. "I'd rather choose an adventure for myself, one without a dragon in it."

Rye suggested, "We could tell the witch to forget about loaning you the sword and go home. We could tell Sir Pinsky he's on his own with the dragon."

Barley didn't say anything for a while. Then he said, "No, all those people are counting on us. The whole kingdom is counting on us. Do you really think Sir Pinsky can fight that dragon on his own?"

Rye couldn't help a small laugh escaping from his throat at the thought of Sir Pinsky trying to fight a dragon with nothing but his own ordinary sword. Hopefully the witch would let them borrow the sword, and hopefully Sir Pinsky would be able to use it. But if not… "Don't worry, Barley. If Sir Pinsky can't use the sword, I'll fight the dragon for you."

"You would?" Barley sounded terrified and relieved at the same time.

"I would," Rye said, terrified, and not at all relieved.

END of Episode Seven

EPISODE EIGHT: THE DRAGON OF THE DEEP

ONE

The next morning the Witch of Lost Castle summoned her three human guests to the throne room. There above her throne, as it had been yesterday, hung the magic sword.

"Sir Pinsky, Knight of the Land Far Away, take my magic sword down from the wall," the Witch of Lost Castle commanded. Her eyes glittered sharp and shrewd in her wrinkled face.

"As you say." Sir Pinsky gave her a small nod, then stepped behind the throne and reached for the sword. He gripped the handle with both hands and, with great difficulty, lifted it from the two hooks that held it in place. "It's rather heavy, isn't it?" Sir Pinsky puffed as he tried to lower it slowly.

Barley sighed. Rye frowned. The magic wasn't working for Sir Pinsky at all.

"Come around where I can see you," the witch said.

Sir Pinsky obediently staggered in front of the witch's throne. His arms shook as he tried to hold up the sword.

"Sir Pinsky, why do you hold that sword in your hand?" the witch asked.

"Because you asked me to take it down from the wall?" Sir Pinsky seemed confused by the witch's question.

"No, no, no. Why do you wish to wield this sword?" the witch asked.

"To slay the Dragon of the Deep," Sir Pinsky said.

"And why do you want to slay the dragon?" the witch asked.

"Because my king commands it." The sword still trembled in Sir Pinsky's hands, as if it was so heavy he was about to drop it.

"Is that all?" the witch prompted.

Sir Pinsky moaned and let the tip of the sword drop to the ground. "Must there be another reason?"

"No." The witch leaned back in her throne. "But I don't believe you. You're not going to fight the dragon only because your king commands it. You're doing it because you want to uphold your honor. You want to prove yourself. You want the fame and the glory, to be the legendary knight who finally slew the Dragon of the Deep."

"Well, yes, all that would be nice too," Sir Pinsky said.

"No!" The witch stood up, her face stern. She pointed a bony finger at Sir Pinsky's chest. "You must clear your mind of all of that. You must not think of yourself at all. The sword will only fight for you if you fight on behalf of others. For your king, for your people, even for young Barley here, who is afraid that if you can't wield this sword, he will have to fight the dragon himself."

"Do you mean I must fight the dragon so that this child does not have to?" Sir Pinsky asked.

Barley gasped, pointing. "Look, Sir Pinsky, you're doing it!"

And so he was. The sword in Sir Pinsky's hand had risen from the floor and now hung steady in the air. Sir Pinsky stared in wonder at it. His arms no longer strained to hold it up. He moved the sword as if it was light as a feather.

"Ah, very good. It worked." The witch plopped back on her throne with satisfaction. "Now, remember exactly how you feel and what you're thinking right now. If you do, the sword will fight the dragon for you. I now loan this magic sword to you on behalf of my good friend Barley Fields of Humble Village, so that you can slay the Dragon of the Deep in Barley's place. When you have finished your task, bring the sword back to me."

"Thank you." Sir Pinsky bowed. "I shall do so."

Two

The journey back to the king's castle was a happy one for Barley and Sir Pinsky. What happened in the witch's throne room had somehow cemented their friendship. Barley begged Sir Pinsky to tell the stories of all his knightly adventures, and Sir Pinsky happily obliged. Rye didn't think that any of these adventures were very exciting. Most ended in a narrow escape of some kind after Sir Pinsky realized he was outmatched by whatever troll or evil wizard or band of brigands he had challenged. He wasn't the best fighter, but he was very, very good at retreating. He might get along well with Soldier Jack, Rye thought.

Sir Pinsky wore the magic sword at his side all the way home. Every day he practiced drawing it out and holding it up. Some days it took a lot of concentration for him to be able to lift it easily, but by the time they had reached King's Town he had gotten very good at it. Barley seemed very pleased that it was for him that Sir Pinsky was wielding the sword. Rye, on the other hand, felt mostly useless. He tried to be grateful that his brother wouldn't be in danger, and that Barley would still get to be a knight, but most of all Rye thought he would simply be glad to go home after this was all over.

The first time they had arrived at King's Town there had been an impromptu parade. This time, the king's fastest messengers had been awaiting them on the road and had

gone ahead to announce their coming. A great crowd of
cheering people met them outside the gates. Trumpets
sounded and drums beat in time as rows upon rows of the
king's soldiers marched them through the streets. Sir Pinsky
drew the magic sword and held it high, and the crowd
shouted in wonder. Rye noticed, even if no one else did, that
Sir Pinsky lowered the sword almost at once and had quite a
bit of trouble getting it back in its sheath. Rye got a terrible
sinking feeling in his stomach. Maybe this wasn't going to
work out at all.

Instead of riding straight for the castle as they had done
when the messenger had first brought them to King's Town,
Barley, Rye, and Sir Pinsky rode all around the streets.
Everywhere they went the people clapped, cheered, and
threw flowers. Rye didn't notice any of it. He was too
worried about Sir Pinsky facing the dragon.

When they finally reached the throne room, the king
welcomed them warmly.

"Show us the sword," King Hugric commanded.

Rye wasn't sure if Sir Pinsky would be able to pull it out.

Nervously, Sir Pinsky glanced around the room. He
seemed to be thinking the very same thing. "First, Your
Majesty, I ask a favor of you before I go and face the
dragon."

"Yes, certainly, ask what you will," King Hugric said.

"This is what I ask. I beg of you, Your Majesty, that you
give me no reward for slaying the Dragon of the Deep. No
honor. No fame. Let it not even be remembered that I did
this deed. Any reward that would have been for me, I ask
you to give it to this boy, Barley Fields of Humble Village.
The use of this sword is his by right by the valor of the deed
he has already accomplished with it. I only wield it to spare
him the danger of facing the dragon. When the story is told,

let it be said that Barley Fields of Humble Village slew the Dragon of the Deep."

The room was silent for a long moment.

"This is an unusual request," King Hugric said, his voice soft but full of emotion. "An unusual and noble request."

Sir Pinsky shook his head. "No, Your Majesty, not even any praise for this request, I beg of you."

"Very well then," King Hugric said. "Your request is granted. Let it be known that all reward and honor for this deed goes to Barley Fields of Humble Village. The name of Sir Pinsky shall never be mentioned in connection with it, henceforth and forever."

"Thank you," Sir Pinsky said. He smiled with relief then put his hand on the hilt of the sword. It came smoothly from its sheath and swung high in the air. There it gleamed in a shaft of sunlight streaming in through a high window. The assembly in the throne room gasped and clapped their hands.

Barley cheered and jumped up and down. "You did it! You did it!"

Perhaps, Rye thought, Sir Pinsky wasn't such a useless knight after all.

"Barley Fields, come forward," King Hugric called.

Barley stepped up to the throne, now looking a little sheepish. Behind him, Sir Pinsky held the sword high, with two hands, right in front of his face, as if in a kind of salute.

"Kneel," the king said and drew his own sword.

Barley went down on one knee. His travel cloak draped to the floor around him. An ache of longing gripped Rye's heart, but he also felt a surge of pride as he watched the king tap Barley on either shoulder.

"I hereby dub you Sir Barley Fields of Humble Village, Knight of the Land Far Away."

THREE

A large crowd came to watch Sir Pinsky battle the dragon. Barley and Rye stood near the king at the front. Everyone kept a safe distance from the water. Sir Pinsky wore his full armor with the magic sword at his side. He bowed to the king, shook hands with Barley, thumped Rye on the shoulder, then turned and marched to the riverbank. A long wooden dock had once stretched out onto the water, but the dragon had splintered the end of it, leaving only a few broken pillars leaning out of the river. Sir Pinsky stepped out to the edge of what was left of the dock and drew the magic sword. He shouted over the water, "Dragon, come forth! I challenge you."

A great white bubble broke the water's surface in the middle of the river. The crowd gasped and cried out in fear. More bubbles came and waves lapped at the shore. A terrible, scaly green head rose up from the water, with eyes like twin moons and a mouth the size of a castle gate.

The mouth grinned.

"Barley," Rye said as a sudden wave of horror flooded over him. "I've just thought of a problem. I don't think the dragon's standing. I think he's swimming."

Barley gasped. He was off like a shot before Rye or the king or anyone could stop him. "Sir Pinsky, watch out! Back up! Make him come on shore!" Barley shouted as he ran toward the broken dock.

"Barley, come back!" Rye started forward, but several hands reached out from the crowd and held him back. "Let me go!" Rye struggled. "Barley! No!"

"Sir Pinsky! Sir Pinsky!" Barley cried.

Sir Pinsky didn't turn around. He had his sword raised, his face turned toward the head of the dragon that came bobbing and swaying as the long green body snaked across the river surface behind it.

"Sir Pinsky, retreat!" Barley shouted.

Sir Pinsky turned for only an instant. "Get back!" he said angrily to Barley, then faced the dragon. The dragon made a playful snap at Sir Pinsky with huge jaws, and Sir Pinsky swung his sword at the long green neck and missed. The crowd cried out in disappointment.

"Get that child off the field of combat!" the king ordered. Several soldiers ran after Barley, but Rye could see they wouldn't reach him before Barley reached Sir Pinsky. Rye fought harder to free himself from the hands that held him back, but could not get loose.

The dragon glanced at Barley. Its round eyes lit up. It darted past Sir Pinsky, shot alongside the dock like a streak of green lighting, and snatched Barley off the ground with a webbed claw.

Rye held his breath. The dragon was on its feet now. Now maybe Sir Pinsky could kill it before Barley got hurt. Sir Pinsky let out a great battle cry and swung his sword toward the dragon's arm as if to chop it off and free Barley, but the dragon reached out his other claw and picked up Sir Pinsky. The sword swung through nothing but empty air as the dragon slid back into the river with his captives. Barley, Sir Pinsky, the sword, and the dragon vanished under the waves in a blink. A great splash went up in the air, a slap of water hit the shore, and then everything was still.

FOUR

"No!" Rye shouted. He sank to the ground, sobbing, staring at the place where the dragon had disappeared. The hands that held him loosened their grip, and Rye pulled away and stumbled toward the water. One of the soldiers stopped him.

"Let me go." Rye beat on the man's uniform coat with his fists. "Let me go, let me go."

"Steady, boy, I can't let you near the water," the soldier said, firm but kind.

The crowd's cries of surprise and horror gradually turned to angry murmurs.

"My people!" the king shouted out. "Listen to me!"

Rye didn't want to listen to the king. How had the king let this happen? Even worse, how had Rye let this happen? Rye never thought that Barley would go charging up to Sir Pinsky to warn him. If Rye had known that, he wouldn't have said anything. He covered his face with his hands and knelt in the tall grass.

The crowd quieted as the king spoke. "Today we have witnessed a tragic event. We had all hoped that we had found a weapon that could defeat the dragon, but alas, it was not to be. Do not give up. Do not give in to despair. We will find a way to drive this dragon from the river, and those who have lost their lives today will not have died in vain."

As the king neared the end of his speech the crowd began to murmur in amazement. Rye looked up to see them all nudging one another and pointing toward the river. Impossible hope surged in his heart. He turned to the water, wishing to see a miracle.

Instead, he saw ducks. A mother duck followed by five little baby ducks swam along the riverbank. He searched for something else, something that the crowd might be so interested in, but saw nothing.

The crowd moved closer to the water, tentatively at first, but then with more confidence.

"Wait," the king said. "Be cautious." He was watching the ducks too.

"They're only ducks," Rye said bitterly.

"There haven't been ducks on the water since the dragon came," said the soldier who had kept Rye from running to the river's edge. "They're swimming out there, bold as you like, and the dragon hasn't snatched them yet."

Rye turned his face away. He didn't think he could bear to see anything else snatched by the dragon.

But the dragon never came. More ducks flew down and settled on the water until there was a whole crowd of them. Nothing disturbed them. The people came closer and closer to the river until they all stood on the very edge, watching the ducks dive and dabble. Some in the crowd even began tossing them bits of bread, which the ducks gobbled up happily.

"It does seem possible that the dragon has been slain after all," The king said. "It is too soon to tell, of course. I recommend that we still exercise caution, but this is a good sign. A very good sign."

FIVE

By nightfall there were all sorts of birds on the river, and small boats too had begun to venture out. Fishermen called to each other, happy to be at work again. The king and all his soldiers went back to the castle, the people went back to the town, and no one seemed to notice that one boy with dark hair and a thin, clever face had gone to sit all alone at the end of the broken dock where Sir Pinsky had faced the dragon.

Rye sat there all night long. He wasn't sleepy, or hungry, or cold. He only wanted to stare into the water and wish his brother was beside him. Rye felt like he had been turned to stone, like he would never move from that spot again. It surprised Rye when the dawn of the next day lit the sky, as if the darkness of that night should have gone on forever.

A voice behind him startled him. "Rye Fields?" It was a quiet and respectful voice, and so it surprised Rye even more to turn around and see the king's messenger, the one who had first come to Humble Village in search of the hero who had defeated the Lord of Lost Castle.

The man's haughty look was gone. Instead, his long face was sad. "King Hugric has a message for you. He wanted me to tell you that since they seem to have defeated the dragon, there is some small hope that your brother, Sir Fields, and Sir Pinsky might have survived. The king has ordered his soldiers to search along the river for any sign of them. He invites you to come to the castle and stay until we have more news."

Rye shook his head. He didn't want to have anything to do with kings or castles. All he wanted was his brother. "No, thank you. I'll wait here."

"I am sorry for what happened," the messenger said, then turned and walked away.

Six

Rye sat alone on the dock for another day and another night. The fishermen knew who he was and what had happened, and one by one they brought him food, or a cup full of water. He hardly touched the food, but the water was welcome.

When dawn came on the second day, Rye had another visitor.

"Hello!" said an unfamiliar but cheerful voice, a boy's voice with a King's Town accent. Rye turned around but couldn't see anyone on the dock or on the shore.

"Hello! I say! Down here!"

The voice came from the water below Rye's feet. Rye looked down and found himself staring into the large, black eyes of a seal.

Rye was not in the mood for a talking seal.

"What you been sitting there all day and all night for?" the seal asked. "Did you lose something?"

"Yes," Rye said. "My brother."

"Oh!" the seal said, not so cheerful anymore. "Oh, I'm terribly sorry. Did he fall in?"

"No, he was snatched in by a dragon," Rye said.

"Oh!" The seal's eyes grew so wide the whites showed around them. "You mean the little yellow-haired boy who was with that fellow with the sword?"

"Yes." Rye leaned out over the dock and stared at the seal. "Do you know what happened to them?"

"Oh, everyone down here knows about that," the seal said. "It's the talk of the whole river. The whole ocean by now. The Dragon of the Deep took a fancy to that boy, that's what he did."

"He didn't..." Rye could hardly bring himself to say it, "...eat him?"

"No, nothing like that." The seal splashed a flipper carelessly across the water's surface. "Took him back to the deeps. Your brother's all cozy in the dragon's palace right now. He'll be safe enough, you can be sure of that."

"He's still alive?" Rye said.

The seal nodded, his nose bobbing just above the water.

"He's not drowned, or eaten?"

"None of those things. And not that fellow that was with him either, the one in all the fancy armor. He's going to be the boy's manservant. Dragon thought the boy would be more comfortable with one of his own kind to wait on him, see?"

Rye's joy at hearing his brother was alive quickly turned to worry. "To wait on him? What does that mean? How long is the dragon going to keep him there?"

"Forever, I guess," the seal said. "Didn't I tell you? That boy, your brother, is to be the dragon's heir. The dragon is making him king of all the ocean someday."

Rye scowled. This seal was making fun of him. "Get out of here."

"Would I joke about something like this?" the seal asked. "If you don't believe me, you can go see for yourself."

"You know very well I can't," Rye said. The seal's story had made him feel worse than ever. Even if what the seal said was true, and Barley was still alive, he was a prisoner of the dragon, and there was nothing Rye could do about it.

"Sure you can go see him," the seal said. "There's a way, if you're willing to make a deal with me."

Rye narrowed his eyes suspiciously. "Is that what this is all about? You want something from me?"

"When I first saw you there, all sorry and sad, I thought maybe you'd dropped your favorite trinket in the river, and I was going to fetch it for you in exchange for a little favor. The conversation went differently than I expected, but yes, I'm talking to you because there's something I want."

"Well, what is it?"

The seal rolled on his back and said wistfully, "I want to go up on shore and walk about in the town, but I need some human clothes to do it in. Can't very well go up there like this." He used a flipper to gesture toward his tail.

"What good would my clothes do you? They won't fit," Rye said. The seal was longer than Rye was tall, and a good deal fatter, and it didn't even have any legs.

"They'll fit if I take my clothes off."

"What clothes?" Rye said.

The seal did the strangest thing then. He pressed a flipper under his chin and the seal's head rolled back like a hood, revealing a boy's impish, pointed face underneath. "I'm a selkie, see?"

Rye scrambled to his feet and backed away in alarm.

"Come on, haven't you heard of selkies? Half human, half seal." The boy's head was all the way out of the sealskin now, and he'd pulled one skinny, white arm free too. "After I'd got your interest by doing you a favor, I was going to offer you a day to play in the river as a seal while I took a stroll through town as a human. As it is, if you trade with me, you can swim out to sea and visit your brother. See for yourself that he's fine and dandy."

"If I put on that sealskin, I can swim out to the ocean and see my brother?" Rye asked.

"Easy as anything," the selkie boy said. "A good day of swimming, and you'll be there by nightfall."

"I don't know the way," Rye said.

"It's to the north once you reach the end of the river. Just ask anyone you meet. Anyone but the sharks, of course. Steer clear of them. They'll eat you soon as soon as look at you. But most folks in the ocean are friendly enough to seals." The selkie boy had wiggled himself all the way out of the sealskin now and was holding it while treading water in the murky river. "Hurry up. It's chilly in here without my skin. Jump in and we'll make the trade."

"I think I'll wade in," Rye said. He took off his socks and shoes and left them on the dock. He had never learned to swim, but he didn't want to admit that to the selkie boy. Watching the water's surface doubtfully, he walked up the dock and jumped in where it was shallow. He waded through the reeds, mud sucking at his feet, until he was in chest-deep. Then he peeled off his wet clothes and handed them to the grinning selkie.

"Thanks!" the selkie said. "Meet you back here in three days. That will give you plenty of time for a nice visit with your brother."

Rye nodded, shaking as much from fear as from the cool river water. He thought about backing out, but if there was any chance the selkie boy was telling the truth, Rye had to go. He had to try and rescue Barley from the dragon.

The sealskin had only one opening at the neck. It stretched wide enough for Rye to pull it up over himself like a rubbery sack. He stuck his arms down the flippers and then the selkie boy, who had already put Rye's clothes on himself, helped Rye pull up the hood. Rye gasped in surprise as he felt the sealskin plump up and tighten. He blinked his new seal's eyes at the strangely bright world around him.

"Now, try out that tail," the selkie boy said.

Rye gave his tail a flip and shot straight into the mud and reeds at the side of the river. He tried to stand up but couldn't get his feet underneath him. They weren't feet anymore, they were fins. Flopping helplessly, he swallowed a mouthful of mud.

"Easy!" the selkie boy laughed. "Look what direction you're going." The selkie boy didn't seem to have any trouble on human legs. He splashed over to Rye and rolled him into deeper waters. "Now, go that direction. And use your flippers to steer. Hold them out like this." The selkie boy held out his right hand to demonstrate. The soaked sleeve of the shirt he'd borrowed from Rye clung tight to the selkie boy's arm. "Do this if you want to go right, this if you want to go left." He dropped his right hand and held out his left one. "Easy enough."

Rye nodded. He carefully made little kicks with his tail until he was out in the middle of the river. He tried putting out his right flipper and began making a circle to the right. Once he was facing the selkie boy again, he let the flipper fall back to his side, and with growing confidence he swam back near the shore.

"You've got it!" the selkie boy cheered. "Don't forget to breathe, at least once an hour, and I'll see you here in three days."

"Three days," Rye nodded, gasping with fear, excitement, and the strangeness of it all. "Which way to the sea?"

The selkie boy groaned and covered his face with one hand. "The way the water's flowing of course, you ignorant human." He pointed down the river.

Rye splashed him with a flipper.

"Get going now." The selkie boy shook his head.

Rye took a deep breath and slid under the water. His new eyes liked the cool, shady river depths. He swam, and swam, and for a very long time felt no need for air. He practiced turning right and left, going up close to the surface, and plunging deep down to the very bottom. As he went, he noticed the river growing deeper and wider. He was on his way to the sea.

END of Episode Eight

Episode Nine: The Sea Prince

ONE

Rye had always wanted a chance to be the hero. After his
brother Barley had rescued him from Lost Castle, he had
wanted it even more. He never imagined how terrified he
would be when it was finally his turn.

In his borrowed sealskin Rye swam down the river until
his whole body ached. He didn't dare slow down. Fear drove
him onward, fear that he wouldn't be able to find the way to
the palace of the Dragon of the Deep, and fear that
something bad might happen to Barley before he got there.

The pain in his muscles grew sharper and Rye's chest
ached as if it would burst. Confused, he tried to keep
swimming, but his body wouldn't listen. He grew weaker
and weaker, until he could hardly wiggle his tail. Then he
remembered he hadn't taken a breath in a long time. The
selkie boy had warned him to breathe at least once an hour.
How long had he been swimming? He had to get to the
surface, or he would drown!

With all the strength he had left, he turned his nose up to
the surface and half swam, half drifted, until he broke out of
the water. The air felt marvelous, pouring into his lungs,
giving him strength. He'd been so worried about Barley he'd
forgotten to breathe.

With his head above the water, Rye saw that the river
would soon open up into a wide bay. Far away near the

horizon rolled the white-capped waves of the ocean. He drank another big breath of air and let it fill him with hope. He had almost reached the sea.

A family of otters floating nearby turned their heads to look at him.

"Hello!" Rye gasped. "Can you tell me how to find the palace of the Dragon of the Deep?"

They shook their heads. "We never go out that far. Better ask one of your own kind."

Rye thanked the otters and headed for the bay. He swam near the surface, gulping air with every few strokes of his tail. The water tasted more and more of salt, and he began to see many different sorts of fish.

"Can you tell me how to find the palace of the Dragon of the Deep?" he asked the fishes, but they only stared at him suspiciously with their big, round eyes and swam away.

"That's right, seals eat fish," Rye muttered as he kept going.

Rye noticed something large and dark in front of him. He went up to the surface and saw a rocky island. Three seals lazed at the edge of the water. Excited, Rye swam closer.

"Hello!" he said. "Can someone tell me how to find the palace of the Dragon of the Deep?"

Three seal heads popped up. They all stared at Rye.

"What's this?" the biggest one asked.

The smallest one stuck his nose out over the water and sniffed. "Looks like Fennly, but it don't sound like Fennly."

"No, I'm not... whoever that is," Rye said.

"Fennly must've swapped clothes with some human pup again," said the middle-sized seal.

"Gone to see his human sweetheart, poor Fennly," the smallest one cooed.

The seals made smooching noises and laughed in short little barks as they rolled side to side on the rocks.

Trying to get their attention, Rye said loudly, "I'm trying to find my brother. I heard the Dragon of the Deep took him to his palace."

The seals fell silent.

"Do you suppose this is the new sea prince's brother?" The largest seal poked the middle one with a flipper and squinted at Rye.

"Does that make him royalty too?" the middle seal asked.

"I don't know," said the smallest seal.

"Hey, human boy, are you on good terms with your brother?" the middle seal asked.

"What?" Rye said.

"Do you suppose he'd be glad to see you? Glad enough that the three kind seals who showed you the way might get invited in for a bite to eat?"

"Yes!" Rye said. "I'm sure my brother will be delighted to see me. In fact, he might hold an entire feast in your honor, to show his gratitude. You could eat to your heart's content." Rye wasn't sure if this was true, but if he could convince these seals to show him the way he could worry about that later.

"Or we might be eaten," the largest seal grumbled. "What if the dragon's feeling hungry? We might look like the main course."

"Two kind seals, then," the middle seal said.

"Count me out. I already did enough swimming today," the smallest seal lay back down on the rock.

"You'll take me there, won't you?" Rye asked the middle seal.

The middle seal took a deep breath and puffed out his chest, held it for a moment, then let it out with a sigh. "These two are right. It's a long way, and dangerous. I'm best off staying here, but I will tell you how to find it. Swim out of the bay and go north. Follow the shore until the land comes to an end. From there, swim straight out to sea toward the North Star. You'll see the lights of the palace beneath you when you get there."

"Please," Rye said, "please come with me and show me the way."

The seal shook his head. "Sorry, human boy, you're on your own."

Two

Sad and anxious, Rye swam away. Ahead of him loomed the great deep of the ocean. Swimming toward it filled him with dread, but he kept going until he had left the bay. The waves rolled him back and forth. He felt in those waves the terrible power of the ocean, a strength that nothing, and especially not one little boy in a borrowed sealskin, could ever hope to resist. Rye swam out far enough that he wouldn't be smashed against the rocks along the shoreline but stayed close enough to shore that he wouldn't be swept away and lost in the vast ocean.

The sun slipped below the distant rim of the ocean, leaving the sky glowing like a dying fire. Rye came around a headland and saw nothing but a long stretch of ocean to his right. The land had come to an end. This was the place. Rye watched the North Star appear in the darkening sky. Without looking back, he swam away from the land, out into the endless waters.

THREE

Everything grew dark and quiet except for the whisper of the waves that rolled around him. Rye felt as if he might be swimming through the night sky, especially when lights began to appear beneath him.

Lights under the water! That meant the dragon's palace lay below him. Rye took a deep, deep breath and dove, quivering with excitement at being so close to the end of his journey.

For a long time, the lights did not seem to get any closer, but then at last Rye could make out strange mounds and tall, twisted towers. Bright lights shone out of the windows, casting a blue glow into the water. Little shrubs in every color of the rainbow covered the walls.

Two large fish swam up from below to meet Rye. At first they were only dark shadows against the lights of the palace. As they approached, Rye could see the gleaming outline of their long snouts that were straight and sharp as swords.

"Who goes there!" one of them shouted.

Rye tried to keep his voice steady and brave. "I'm Rye Fields. I want to see my brother Barley. I heard the Dragon of the Deep took him to his palace."

"Be off with you," the other fish said, pointing his sword nose straight at Rye's heart. "Prince Barley is a human, not a seal. He's no brother of yours."

Prince Barley! So his brother was here. "I'm not a seal," Rye said, feeling braver now that he knew for sure Barley was still alive. "I traded clothes with a selkie boy so I could come and visit my brother. Please let him know I'm here."

"Very well," the first fish said, "But if you are lying the dragon will have you for his midnight snack. Wait here."

The first fish swam down until he disappeared into one of the bright doorways of the palace. The second fish kept his long, sharp nose pointed at Rye. Rye hated having to wait. The vast, cold darkness of water all around him made him shiver inside his sealskin. He began to feel as if he needed a breath. He wanted to ask the palace guard fish if he could swim up to the surface for a moment and then come back, but the fish stared at him so fiercely he didn't dare say anything.

After a long time, the other guard fish came back. "Prince Barley wants to know by what token you will prove to him that you are his brother."

"I don't understand," Rye said. It was hard for him to think about anything except getting a breath of air.

"What do you know that only Prince Barley's brother would know?" the palace guard fish asked.

Rye tried hard to come up with something, but his brain felt like winter molasses. He knew he and Barley lived in Humble Village, he knew Barley had rescued him from Lost Castle, but everyone in the kingdom knew that. A sudden thought came to him, and Rye giggled. "Tell him I put his new shoes in the butter churn."

The guard fish nodded and swam away again. After a while, Rye didn't feel so much as if he needed air anymore. The deep ocean water seemed warmer. It rolled him gently back and forth, the lights of the palace were so beautiful, and the guard fish with his sword for a nose wasn't nearly as frightening as he had been at first. Everything became hazy and bright. Rye thought he saw the other fish guard coming back, a blurry dark shadow against the palace glow, but he wasn't sure. Besides, he couldn't remember why the fish had gone in the first place, or what he was even doing at the bottom of the ocean.

The lights gradually dimmed, and then went out.

Four

"Rye? Can you hear me?"

"Mmmph!" Rye wanted to roll over and pull the covers up over his head. What a horrible dream! About a dragon, and losing Barley, and swimming to the bottom of the ocean. He groped for his blanket, and then realized his arm wasn't working like an arm should. It didn't have an elbow. He couldn't make a fist with his fingers.

He was still a seal.

Rye's eyes shot open. The face staring down at him was Barley's, but it was different. Horrifyingly different. Rye yelped in surprise. His brother's hair hung wet and green around a face that had a few tiny silver-blue scales growing like freckles on the pale pink skin. Small webbed fins stuck out from the edge of Barley's ears. Rye wanted to ask Barley what had happened to him, but before he could, a coughing fit shook his whole body. He belched up a bucketful of water, coughed a few more times, then shut his eyes and moaned.

"Easy there, my boy. You nearly drowned, you know," said another familiar voice.

"Sir Pinsky?" Rye asked hoarsely. He was almost afraid to see what had happened to the knight. When he opened his eyes again, he saw Sir Pinsky smiling down at him. Same ordinary brown hair, plain face, and moustache as always.

Rye turned to Barley, hoping that he had been wrong about the fins and scales. Barley still had green hair, ear fins, and a scattering of scales on his face. He wore fine clothes that shimmered as if they were made of silver.

"Hooray!" Barley gave Rye a hug. "Rye, it really is you, isn't it? Are you going to be a seal now forever? Because then we can be together here in the ocean. I'm so happy to see you!"

Rye blinked and began to take in the room around him. He wasn't underwater anymore, but everything was damp and drippy. White walls made of rough, spongy stone encircled them. Round pearls of all colors and sizes dotted the room. There were no windows. Ripples of light danced over the stone ceiling, shining up from a bright pool in the middle.

"Barley, I…" Rye tried to hug his brother back, but it was hard with only seal fins to do it. "I've only borrowed this sealskin. I have to give it back. And besides, you're coming home with me. I'm here to rescue you." Rye coughed up more sea water.

Sir Pinsky thumped Rye on the back while Barley watched him with concern.

"I'm fine now," Rye said. There was no one else in the room besides Barley and Sir Pinsky. Rye wondered if they could simply slip away now, or if they would need more of a plan in order to escape. "Are we in the palace?"

"Yes," Barley said. "This is a special room the dragon made just for me, in case I got tired of being underwater, since I'm not used to it yet. He's really very kind and generous, once you get to know him."

Rye stared at Barley in confusion. "The dragon is kind? But he wrecked all those boats and ate everyone and everything that went on the river. How can you say he's kind?"

"He was only angry because the king refused to give him what he wanted," Barley said. "He's usually a very nice dragon."

Rye frowned. The king hadn't mentioned that the dragon had asked him for anything. "What are you talking about? What did the dragon want?"

"A human child to come and live with him at the bottom of the ocean and be his heir and someday become king of the sea. All King Ugric had to do was give the dragon what he asked for, and the destruction would have stopped. It was really the king's fault all along."

"The king's fault?" Rye backed away from Barley. "How could it be the king's fault? That's a terrible thing for the dragon to ask! If I were King Ugric, I wouldn't have given a child to that horrible dragon."

"I will have no word spoken against the Dragon of the Deep," Barley said sharply. "He is my father now, and I am his son."

Rye wished he had drowned rather than live to hear Barley say those words. "So it's you. You're the child the dragon took? To be his heir?" Rye couldn't help a sob escaping with his next words. "Are you still my brother?"

"Yes, of course!" Barley said. "I'm so glad you're here. I'm glad you came, though you can see I have no need to be rescued. I'm very safe and happy here. I wish you could stay forever, but since you say you have to go back you can tell Mother and Father that I'm well. I will come and visit them myself, once I'm grown into a dragon."

"Is that what's happening to you?" Rye reached for Barley's face with a flipper. Huge salty tears stung his big seal eyes. Barley had been so afraid of dragons, and now he was turning into one. "Barley, no, you have to come home with me. I told Mother and Father I'd bring you back safely. Please!"

"I don't have to go anywhere," Barley said. "I don't want to go home. I don't want to be a farmer. I don't even want to be a knight. I'm the sea prince, and someday I'll be the king!"

"I thought you wanted to go home," Rye pleaded. "That's what you said that night at Lost Castle. You just wanted this to all be over so we could go home. I came all this way, I nearly drowned, and it was all so I could bring you home."

"I am home, Rye. This is my home now," Barley said. "It could be your home too, if you want."

Rye turned his face away. He didn't want to hear any more.

"Prince Barley, your brother has had a long journey. He must be very tired. Perhaps you should let him rest, and the two of you can... um... discuss this later?" Sir Pinsky suggested.

"Very well," Barley said. "I'm glad you came, Rye. When you're rested, I'll show you around the palace. You'll like it."

Rye shook his head. He was sure he wouldn't like it at all. True, he was exhausted, but Rye didn't think he could rest. Now Rye knew he had been right to worry. Something terrible had happened to Barley, worse than Rye could have ever imagined. Rye didn't know what to do. He had found Barley, but Barley didn't want to be rescued.

"You'll stay with him, Sir Pinsky?" Barley asked.

"Of course," Sir Pinsky said.

"See you soon, Rye," Barley said.

Rye watched sadly as Barley slipped into the bright pool of water and disappeared.

"I've tried to reason with him," Sir Pinsky said as soon as they were alone. "I've tried to convince him that the dragon is not what he thinks. But he will not listen."

"Does the dragon have him under a spell?" Rye asked. "Is there a way to break it?"

"It may be a spell from the dragon, but then again it may not. How many boys in your village would jump at the chance to be a king, to be given the strength and power of a dragon, and to have all the wealth in the sea?"

"I would not!" Rye said. "That dragon does nothing but take things. I would never want to become like him."

"He has taken from you, but to Barley he has given great honor. Be careful. Your brother is not likely to be persuaded by argument."

"Then how will we persuade him?" Rye pleaded. "What can we do?"

"Rest for now," Sir Pinsky said. "Now that you are here, I have more hope that Barley will come to his senses. Rest, and wait. We'll think of something."

END of Episode Nine

Episode Ten: Games with Dragons

ONE

Rye found that he couldn't sleep at all. He tried, but he wasn't comfortable as a big, blubbery seal sausage with flippery arms and no feet. As if that wasn't enough, his head spun with worried thoughts about Barley. He had to find some way to convince Barley to come home, and he didn't have very long to do it. The selkie boy whose sealskin Rye had borrowed would be waiting for Rye at King's Town in two days. If Rye didn't show on time, he didn't know what would happen. Maybe the selkie would decide he liked being human and leave Rye stuck as a seal forever. The thought made Rye moan and roll over on the soggy coral floor.

After a while, Sir Pinsky began to snore. Rye cracked open an eye and glared at him in irritation. If Sir Pinsky had been better at fighting dragons, the Dragon of the Deep might be in little pieces at the bottom of the river, and Barley and Rye would be almost home by now. Rye shook his head at himself and sighed. He shouldn't blame Sir Pinsky. That wouldn't help solve the problem.

Rye needed to think, and to do that he needed to stop feeling like a wet sausage that had been dropped on the floor. He rolled over to the edge of the pool at the middle of the room and slipped into the water. He felt much better with the cool sea all around him. His body moved slowly and gracefully as he swam downward. Through the large, open windows the water glowed a deep blue-green, so Rye guessed that the sun had come up. Tall coral pillars held up the room that Rye had been in, and coral walls covered with swaying sea plants surrounded him on all sides. Colorful fishes swam busily through tunnels and arches in the walls, nodding respectfully to the pair of guards that patrolled lazily by. Through the archways, Rye could see more guards with their long, sharp noses swimming in the water around the palace. Even if he convinced Barley to come with him, they wouldn't be able to escape easily.

"Oh, good! You're awake!" Barley's voice made Rye turn around. It shocked Rye all over again to see Barley's face speckled with small, pearly-blue scales. Rye thought there might be even more scales now than there had been before. "Are you ready to see the palace? You're going to love it!"

The palace, Rye had to admit, was wonderful. Barley led him through chamber after chamber, down long winding tunnels, and through open gardens full of the strange plants of the sea. In one room, piles of treasure that must have come from sunken ships glimmered in the dim undersea light. In another room, heaps of pearls of all sizes lay like so many pebbles on the floor. If Barley stayed, Rye thought, then all of this would be his. No wonder he didn't want to leave.

They passed a large grotto where several of the guards were practicing sword fighting with their lance-like noses. Rye smiled, "I wonder what Soldier Jack would think of this," he said.

"Soldier Jack?" Barley asked, as if he didn't know what Rye was talking about.

"Yes, from our village. He used to give us sword fighting lessons."

"Did he?" Barley said, confused.

Rye studied Barley's pale, scale-spotted face. "Don't you remember Soldier Jack?"

Barley shook his head, then grinned. "It doesn't matter. Dragons don't use swords. We have claws, and teeth, and tails. The Dragon of the Deep is teaching me how to fight with them."

Rye didn't like hearing Barley's usual cheerful enthusiasm behind such terrible words. Barley's teeth did look a little longer and sharper, and so did his fingernails. At least, Rye thought, Barley hadn't started growing a tail yet. Rye had to get Barley out of here before he became even more like a dragon.

They came to a large, open area with a distant coral wall. A few guards swam along it as dark, sharp-nosed shadows in the eternal fog of the sea. "Let's have a swimming race," Barley said. "All the way to the wall and back."

"I don't know," Rye said. He was still sore from all the swimming he'd done yesterday. It had used muscles he didn't know he'd had, and all of them were hurting.

"Come on," Barley said. "The dragon and I race here every day. It's so I can learn to swim faster." Barley showed off the thin webs growing between his fingers and toes.

"I'll race you, then," Rye said, not wanting to be outdone by the dragon for doing things with Barley.

The two of them started off. Rye kicked his tail hard and shot through the water. To his surprise, Barley's laughter followed right beside him. Barley wriggled through the water like a snake, moving so fast that Rye had to swim as hard as he could to keep up with him, even with his own set of flippers and fins.

They reached the wall together, but then after they turned around, by the time Barley reached the castle, Rye had fallen behind. He was running out of air.

"Are you all right?" Barley asked as Rye swam past him through an open arch.

"I need some air," Rye said. "Where's the room?"

Two

Barley led Rye back to the little room high up in the tallest tower of the dragon's palace. As soon as Rye's head burst above the surface, he got a good, deep breath of air. He flipped his tail hard and jumped out of the water, up on the floor. Barley climbed out after him.

"Good race," Rye said, trying to catch his breath.

"I think you might have beat me if you hadn't run out of air," Barley said.

"Maybe," Rye said. "Do you remember running home at supper time after helping father in the fields? That time I pretended the brigands were after us?"

Barley didn't say anything.

Sir Pinsky opened his eyes and sat up, listening.

"You've got to remember," Rye said. "It was the day before we went to pick blackberries, and I was taken to Lost Castle."

Barley frowned and shook his head.

"You remember Lost Castle, don't you?" Rye asked. "And the witch? And where you got the magic sword?"

Barley still looked confused.

"What do you remember?" Sir Pinsky asked.

"I remember the dragon bringing me here," Barley said. "Everything before that is a bit foggy."

"Do you remember mother's sausage pie?" Rye asked.

Barley shrugged apologetically.

This was really serious. Sausage pie had always been Barley's favorite. "You remembered that I put your shoes in the butter churn," Rye said.

"Actually, I remembered that," Sir Pinsky said.

"You?" Rye asked.

"Yes, you two told me the story while we were on our way to Lost Castle," Sir Pinsky said. "When the guard came and told us what you had said, I assured Sir Barley that you must indeed be his brother."

Angry now, Rye turned back to Barley. "How about Old Lumpy?"

"What was lumpy?" Barley asked.

"Our horse!" Rye said.

"Our horse was lumpy?" Barley asked in disbelief.

"His name was Lumpy," Rye said. "You can't have forgotten Lumpy. He brought us to the king's castle. He's in the royal stables, waiting for us to take him home."

"I suppose you'll have to take him on your own then," Barley said.

"I don't want to take him home without you," Rye said.

"This is my home now," Barley said. "And this is where I'm going to stay."

No wonder Barley didn't want to go home. It wasn't only because he thought the dragon was his friend or because of the fantastic palace he got to live in and would inherit someday. The real problem was that Barley couldn't remember what his real home was like. Rye closed his eyes and tried to think of what he'd said to help his friends remember home when they were locked in the dungeon of Lost Castle. "There's a road, and a well, and houses with daubed walls and thatched roofs. There's fields all around, and gardens, and apple trees. You can hear sheep bells, and cowbells, and the smith's hammer, and the mill wheel creaking."

Rye opened his eyes to see if it was working. Barley was listening, but with a blank expression on his face.

Rye kept talking. "We would ride through the village first. The goodwives would look up from sweeping their porches or hanging out their washing and call out a welcome. All our friends, Jep and Tildy Weaver, Tom Cobbler, Janet, all of them would come running to greet us then run home even faster to tell their families of our safe return. On the far side of the village, the sun would be low over the fields, the first haystacks would be standing by rows of uncut grass, and in the long shadows you'd feel the first hint of autumn coming on. We'd round a bend and there would be a little whitewashed cottage with a mossy thatched roof and a string of smoke coming out the chimney. You'd smell stew cooking, full of sweet vegetables from the garden, and bread baking. Then there would be a happy shout that warms you right down to your toes. It would be Father. He'd have spied us coming, and he'll throw down his rake and leap the fence to meet us in the road. Mother would run out of the house, laughing and crying for joy, and you'd jump down off Old Lumpy's back, right into her arms."

Sir Pinsky sniffled a little and wiped away a tear.

Barley sat, wide-eyed and stunned, with his bare webbed feet dangling in the water. "I remember now," he said. "I remember everything." He looked straight at Rye, a terrible ache of longing in his face. "I want to go home."

THREE

Barley hugged Rye tight around his rubbery seal neck and cried tears into Rye's seal whiskers. Rye patted his back as best he could with one wet seal flipper.

"I knew you could do it, Rye," Sir Pinsky said. "That's half the battle won already."

"As for the other half," Rye said, "I still don't know what to do. There's guards everywhere. If we try to run, or... actually... swim away, we'll be caught."

"No need to run away," Barley said. "I'll just tell the dragon I want to go home."

"Do you think he'll let you leave? Just like that?" Rye asked.

"Yes, I think he will," Barley said. He rubbed away the last of his tears. "Trust me. You don't know the dragon like I do. He's really very nice."

Sir Pinsky shook his head.

"I don't think we should mention this to the dragon. Let's try and come up with a plan on our own," Rye said.

Barley folded his arms stubbornly. "We can at least try asking nicely," he said. "If the dragon says no, then we'll come up with some other plan."

"If the dragon says no and doesn't lock us all up somewhere," Rye said. "Or eat us."

"He would never do that! He says I'm like a son to him. He told me I could have anything I wanted, and if I want to go home then I'm sure he'll let me go."

"If you're sure," Rye said. They could try and talk to the dragon, Rye thought, but he didn't think the dragon was likely to let them go easily. Rye determined to be on the lookout for another plan.

FOUR

The Dragon of the Deep held court in a magnificent coral chamber. At the center, a gigantic empty clam shell gleamed with pale pink mother-of-pearl. It rested on a tall pillar encrusted with gemstones and gold from sunken ships. More treasure lay piled in the bowl of the shell. The dragon coiled lazily over it with his long white mane flowing in the water.

"Welcome, Prince Barley of the Deep. Welcome, Rye, brother of the prince," the dragon's voice echoed, deep and musical, through the chamber. He nodded to Rye. "We are very glad to have you as our guest."

"Thank you," Rye said, noticing that the dragon had no wings. None at all. It had front legs, back legs, a long tail with webbed fins running down it, but no wings. The Dragon of the Deep couldn't fly.

That was useful to know.

"Begging your pardon, my father," Barley said with his head bowed. "I have a request."

"What is this request, my son," the dragon asked.

"I wish to go home to my mother and father on land. I want to return to Humble Village."

A deep growl rumbled in the dragon's throat. "I see your brother has come here to turn you against me." The dragon bared his long, sharp teeth as his yellow eyes fixed on Rye. "I welcomed you into my palace as my guest, but you have betrayed me by seeking to rob me of my only son."

Rye shuddered inside his sealskin. His heart beat so fast he thought it would go to pieces. And then he saw something near the rim of the dragon's shell throne. Among gold cups and crowns lay a gleaming sword with gems on the handle. The magic sword. The witch's sword, the one Barley had borrowed to slay the dragon. When Rye saw that sword, an idea came into his head.

"Would you agree to a contest?" Rye said.

"A contest for what?" The dragon uncoiled from his throne. He swam toward Rye, teeth still bared.

"A contest for Barley. If I win, he comes home with me. If you win, he stays."

"And why should I agree to this contest?" the dragon said. "I could eat all of you now and find another human child willing to come to the deep with me. There must be dozens, hundreds, who would be happy to trade a life of misery up on land for one of wealth and glory and beauty down here in the sea."

"Then why not just let me go?" Barley asked angrily. "If you can replace me so easily, just let me go!"

The dragon's eyes shut half-way. He slowly coiled back on his throne. After a long silence, the dragon asked, "What is this contest?"

"A game of hide and seek," Rye said. "Barley and I, and Sir Pinsky, will have three days to hide something. That sword perhaps, the one Sir Pinsky was using, when… well, you know." Rye glanced at Sir Pinsky, who had a pained and anxious look on his face. "Anyway, we'll hide the sword, and then you have to find it. You can have three days too, if you like. If you find the sword, Barley will return to the deep with you. If you don't find it, you have to go back alone, and you are to never come on the land or up the river again."

The dragon laughed. "I am like lightning in the water and thunder on the land. There is nowhere you can hide this sword that I will not find it in three days' time."

"Then you agree to this contest?" Rye asked.

"I agree," said the dragon. His yellow eyes flashed wide, and his teeth opened in a terrible grin. "You may begin NOW!" The last word turned into a roar that shuddered the coral walls. He flicked the sword off the edge of his throne with a single claw and stared at Rye while it sank to the floor and stuck point down into the sand.

FIVE

Rye wasted no time getting to the sword. He gripped the
handle in his mouth and pulled it free. It was an awkward
thing to carry. It hurt his teeth and slowed him down when
he tried to swim.

Barley shot through the water to Rye's side. "Let me take
that," Barley said. "You help Sir Pinsky. He can't swim very
fast."

Barley slid the sword into his belt with an angry frown
on his face. The dragon sat curled on his throne, chin resting
on one claw, watching the three of them with a very amused
expression.

"Put your arms around my neck," Rye said as he swam
up to Sir Pinsky. "Hold on tight."

Sir Pinsky nodded and wrapped his arms around Rye.
Rye felt a little choked, but it wasn't as bad as trying to swim
with the heavy sword in his mouth.

"This way," Barley led them toward an open archway at
the side of the throne room. The guards drew aside to let
them pass. As Rye swam out of the palace and upward to the
surface of the ocean, he could hear the dragon laughing
behind him.

What Rye thought might be late evening twilight over
the ocean above them turned out to be heavy clouds and

rain. A fierce wind blew the waves into high hills with white crests.

"I hope you've got a very good idea of where to hide that sword," Sir Pinsky said with a cough and a shudder as soon as they were out into the open air.

"I think I know what he has in mind," Barley said with a big grin for Rye.

Rye grinned back, though it felt funny grinning with his seal's face.

"Now, which way is the land?" Barley asked Rye.

Rye's heart sank. He hadn't thought about that. They couldn't see the sun or the stars. Nothing but waves and wind all around. They would have to wait until the storm was over, and that could take days. The dragon had won already. Perhaps the dragon knew about the storm, and that's why he had been laughing.

"I don't know," Rye said. "There's no way to tell."

"That way," Sir Pinsky let go of Rye's neck with one arm and pointed. "The storms on the sea always blow from the west this time of year, so south is that direction, and south is where the land lies."

"Hooray for Sir Pinsky!" Barley said. "He knows the way."

It would have been easier to swim beneath the waves, but then they would have had no sense of direction at all. They had to stay up where they could feel the wind, even though the swells tossed them up and down and made swimming twice as exhausting. The sky grew darker, and soon they could see nothing. Barley held onto Sir Pinsky's foot while Sir Pinsky held onto Rye so that they wouldn't lose each other in the storm.

After it seemed like hours and hours had passed, Barley called out over the wind, "Rye, stop! I hear something."

Rye stopped and tried to keep his head above the waves so he could hear with his tiny seal ears. When he kept still, he could feel something. Something had changed about the water. He sensed a rumble and hiss, and now and then a great thunderous crash.

"I think it might be the shore," Rye said.

"I think you're right. We're almost there," Barley said. "Let's go!"

"Wait," Sir Pinsky said. "We can't go ashore blind like this. It's too dangerous. The waves could crush us on rocks before we know what's happening. I've seen ships broken to pieces in better weather than this."

It was terrible, waiting and listening in the blackness. Every moment was precious. Rye wondered why he hadn't asked the dragon for more time to hide the sword, perhaps a whole week instead of only three days.

At last the rain stopped and the sound of breaking waves became clearer. Rocks, or cliffs, waited somewhere ahead of them in the dark. Then the clouds thinned, and a few patches of moonlight shone down onto the rolling sea. A dark wall loomed up out of the sea ahead of them, with surging splashes of white at the base.

"There's the land!" Barley said, excited.

"Yes, but there's something wrong," Rye said. The sea cliffs stretched as far as he could see in both directions. There should have been a way for them to continue south around a headland. "I don't know where we are."

"Let's go find out," Barley said.

They swam toward the sea cliffs, searching for a safe place to go ashore. At first Rye insisted that they swim westward into the wind, looking for the end of the cliffs that he had passed on his way to the dragon's palace, but they found that they couldn't go in that direction. The wind was too strong. Instead they swam east, with the wind, in hopes of finding a place where the waves weren't so fierce and the cliffs not so steep.

The sun was coming up by the time the cliffs parted to make way for a small bay. A town stood near the water and a crowd of tall-masted ships huddled around the long docks, all of it dark and wet from the storm.

As soon as they entered the bay the wind wasn't so strong, and the waves weren't so high. Sir Pinsky let go of Rye's neck and swam for himself. At last, all three of them crawled or flopped up onto the sand, exhausted.

"Do you still have the sword?" Rye murmured, too tired to raise his head and look.

"Got it," Barley said weakly from somewhere nearby.

"Good," Rye said. He knew they ought to keep moving, but there wouldn't be any harm in lying still for a minute. He was so very, very tired. He shut his eyes and, completely by accident, fell fast asleep.

END of Episode Ten

Episode Eleven: Things Lost and Found

ONE

A familiar, friendly voice woke Rye from sleep. "Sir Barley
Fields!" the voice boomed. "How did you come to be lying
on this beach?"

Rye opened his eyes. The bald-headed merchant from
Oakbridge Crossing stood beside them in the sand. Today
the merchant wore a long red coat with gold trim and gold
buttons, and he had a crowd of curious people at his back.

Barley jumped up. "It's you!" he shouted and hugged
the merchant around his large middle. "How did you find
us?"

"Last night I heard the sad tale of your disappearance
into the river, and that the king of the Land Far Away had
called for a search," the merchant said. "And then this
morning all the talk of the town was that a man, a boy, and a
seal had come swimming in out of the storm and crawled up
on the beach. I thought it might be you. I'm very pleased to
see that I was correct!" The merchant thumped Barley on the
back. "Though you are a bit changed since we last met."

Barley stuck his webbed fingers into his pockets and
lowered his eyes.

The merchant set his hand on Barley's shoulder. "Your
brother will be very happy to hear that you're alive. The last
I heard he was sitting on the end of a dock and watching the
river as if hoping you might return."

"Oh, Rye knows I'm all right," Barley said. "He's right there." He pointed at Rye, who had raised his head and was holding himself up on his flippers.

The merchant frowned. "Unless I'm very much mistaken, the last time we met your brother was not a seal."

"I borrowed this sealskin from a selkie boy, so I could go and look for Barley at the palace of the Dragon of the Deep," Rye said.

The merchant and everyone behind him gasped and stepped back when Rye spoke.

"Yes," Barley said. "Rye came and rescued me from the dragon!"

A murmur of amazement ran through the crowd.

"A selkie, did you say?" the merchant asked, with a grin for Rye. "That's clever, my boy."

Rye gasped. "Oh no! I forgot. I have to take this sealskin back to the selkie by tomorrow. I promised I would. He'll be waiting for me by the river, at the dock where Sir Pinsky fought the dragon."

"Will we have time to hide the sword and take the sealskin back too?" Barley asked.

"That depends on where we are right now," Rye said. He asked the merchant, "I'm afraid we got lost on our way back from the dragon's palace. I wanted to swim back to King's Town, but the storm blew us here instead. Where are we?"

"This is the Bay of Ayr, in the Rose Grove Kingdom. There you see the Town of Ayr, and the Port of Ayr, where a ship is being laden to carry my goods to all the Emerald Realms," the merchant said proudly.

"I should have asked the dragon for more time!" Rye flopped on the sand and tried to bury his head under his flippers. The flippers didn't quite reach. "If we're all the way in the Rose Grove Kingdom we'll never make it."

"Hello." Sir Pinsky nervously brushed the sand off of himself as best he could, then went and shook hands with the merchant. "I am Sir Pinsky, and lately the traveling companion of these two young gentlemen."

"Pleased to make your acquaintance. I am Vendan Tropp of Oakbridge Crossing, traveling merchant, and your young companions did me a great favor not too long ago by defeating the Lord of Lost Castle."

"I beg your pardon for asking, but would you be willing to do us a favor in return?" Rye asked the merchant.

"If it can be done, it shall be done," the merchant said.

Rye looked around at all the people standing on the beach. He didn't want to give away the secret of where he planned to hide the sword, in case any creature might be listening who would tell the dragon. Rye lowered his voice. "Is there somewhere we can go to talk in private?"

"Of course," the merchant said. He turned to the crowd. "Thank you, everyone. I will be taking charge of these two boys and their waterlogged knight. You may now go about your business."

The crowd faded away reluctantly, with many curious glances over their shoulders, especially at Barley. Though he had stuck his webbed fingers into his pockets and tried to bury his webbed toes in the sand, he couldn't hide the fins on his ears or the handful of scales that speckled his face.

"Come with me," the merchant said. "We can talk in my room at the inn."

Rye tried to follow the merchant up the beach, but after a few clumsy attempts to move, he flopped forward onto his face. He had learned to swim like a seal, but he had no idea how to move around on land. Right now, there was no time to figure it out.

"Wait," Rye said. "I can't go very fast like this on land." Rye wondered if Barley, Sir Pinsky, and the merchant all working together might be able to carry him. He wasn't sure.

"Can't you take it off?" the merchant asked.

"I haven't tried yet," Rye said. "I saw the selkie boy take it off. He put his flipper under his chin, like this, and off came the seal's head, easy as pulling back a hood."

"Give it a try, then," Barley said.

Rye pushed up on his chin with his flipper. It was awkward since he had to bend his head around before his flipper could even reach. He poked and pushed until finally the sealskin split open a little, and Rye could feel the cool sea air on his human throat. "It's going!" Rye said, and tried using both flippers to pry the head off the rest of the way.

Barley got behind him, grabbed under Rye's chin, and pulled up. With the two of them working together the seal's head slid back and hung loose behind Rye's neck. Rye blinked his eyes. Everything looked dim and gray without his sharp seal eyes that could see even in the underwater world. It was a relief to be out of the seal head, to have his own face again, but Rye felt a prick of loss as well.

The merchant took off his coat and handed it to Rye. Rye wiggled the rest of the way out of the sealskin and wrapped the coat around himself like a big red and gold robe.

"It's good to see you again, Rye," Barley said with a smile.

"It's good to be myself." Rye shifted his weight from one foot to the other, enjoying how the sand felt on his bare feet. He bent down, scooped up the heavy, wet sealskin, and held it carefully against his chest. "We have to hurry now. We only have two days left to beat the dragon."

Two

Vendan Tropp, the bald-headed merchant from Oakbridge Crossing, led Rye, Barley, and Sir Pinsky at a brisk walk up the beach and into the streets of town. In the town of Ayr, roses grew everywhere: in the hedges, in window-boxes, trained up walls and around doorways. The people dressed in bright colors and men and women alike had roses embroidered into their clothes. The salt air of the sea mingled with the sweet scent of the flowers. Rye's lungs weren't big enough to breathe in as much of it as he wanted.

They came to a tall building on a corner with a sign that said, "Ayr Harbor Inn." A hedge of roses ran snugly around the base of the inn and shaded a bower leading up to the door. Merchant Tropp led them inside, up the stairs, and to a room at the end of the hall with a wide bay window looking over the harbor.

"Shut the door," Rye said. "Close all the curtains."

When the door was shut and all the curtains closed, and Barley had peeked under the door to make sure no one was standing out in the hall, everyone gathered around Rye.

"We have two days to hide this sword somewhere that the Dragon of the Deep can't find it," Rye said. "There's only one place I know of that'll be safe, and that's at Lost Castle."

"Indeed," the merchant said. "The dragon will never find it there. Only one problem. How are *you* going to find Lost Castle?"

"We know how!" Barley said. "All we need is some cheese. And bread."

The merchant chuckled. "Miraculous. Marvelous. Granted. I can supply you with all the cheese and bread you could wish for."

"We also need transportation," Rye said. "How far are we from Lost Forest here?"

"Only a few hour's ride from the northern edge. Lost Forest lies on the border between the Rose Grove Kingdom and the Land Far Away."

"We're close then!" Rye said. "Even closer than if I'd taken us back by way of the river."

"We'll have nearly two days to find the castle. We can still do it," Barley said.

"If nothing else goes wrong," Sir Pinsky nodded.

"And how far are we from King's Town in the Land Far Away?" Rye asked.

"A full day's hard riding," Merchant Tropp said. "There's a road through Lost Forest, and then across the plains, over the river, and you're there."

Rye looked down at the sealskin in his hands. "I can ride to King's Town while Barley and Sir Pinsky look for Lost Castle."

"No, leave the sealskin for later," Barley said. "We have to hide the sword first!"

"No," Rye said. "I have to keep my word. I'll take the sealskin back to the selkie boy, then I'll meet you at Lost Castle. Do you remember how to find it, Barley?"

Barley nodded. "I'll ask the birds."

"Oh, not this again," Sir Pinsky said. "Perhaps I should accompany you instead, Rye."

"No, Sir Pinsky, please go with Barley. If something else does go wrong, if you can't find the castle, you'll have to fight the dragon," Rye said.

Sir Pinsky did not like the sound of that.

"You'll be able to do it this time," Barley said. "The only reason the magic sword didn't work last time was because the dragon was swimming, not standing."

"Very well, then. I will accompany Sir Barley, and, if needed, I will defend him from the dragon with my life."

Merchant Tropp spread a large map over the table. "I will show you the routes you should take and the towns and stables where you can get a fresh horse once you reach the far side of the forest, Rye. I'll also give you a letter stating that any charges you incur at stable or inn will be paid by me. Consider your adventure financed."

"Thank you," Rye said.

"Thank you!" Barley gave the merchant another hug.

THREE

Rye studied the map while Vendan Tropp sent for some breakfast and some sensible traveling clothes for all three of them. By mid-morning, Barley, Rye, and Sir Pinsky were galloping down the south road. Barley had a pack filled with the best cheese and finest bread to be found in the town of Ayr, useful for tempting the helpful squirrels and birds of Lost Forest. Sir Pinsky had a new sword belt and sheath to carry the magic sword. Rye's pack held the selkie boy's sealskin, as well as food, water, and the letter from Merchant Tropp.

As they rode, Rye went over and over it in his mind, trying to find some way for him to reach Lost Castle before the dragon came looking for the sword. He had a feeling that the dragon might come looking for him too, and that if the dragon found him there wouldn't be much to keep the dragon from swallowing him whole, just out of spite. If the selkie boy was there at the dock waiting for him, and then after handing off the sealskin he rode for Lost Forest as fast as he could, would he be able to find the castle in time?

The edge of Lost Forest appeared in the distance like a dark green haze covering the hills. They rode together all the way up to where the trees made an archway over the road, and then they rode a little farther together into the darkness of the forest.

"You two should start looking," Rye said, though he didn't dare say for what out loud. "I'll ride on to King's Town."

"Are you sure you can't wait a few more days to give the sealskin back?" Sir Pinsky asked.

"Yes, Rye, I wish you would come with us," Barley said. "I'll be so worried."

"I don't know what will happen if I don't keep my word," Rye said. "It's not good to trifle with the promises you make to magical creatures."

"True," Sir Pinsky said. "All too true. Be careful, Rye."

Rye checked all around to make sure no creature was in sight. The forest lay silent. He leaned close to Barley and lowered his voice to a whisper. "Tell the witch to have her animal friends watching for me. I'll need someone to show me the way as soon as I get back to the forest."

"I will," Barley said.

Rye wanted to give his little brother a hug, this was maybe the last chance they would ever have to embrace, but to do that they would have to get off their horses and there didn't seem to be enough time as it was. He reached a hand out instead and Barley clasped it tight in his own.

"Thank you for coming to rescue me," Barley said. "I told you that you would get a chance."

"I guess we're even now," Rye said.

"I'm not entirely rescued yet," Barley said. "First we have to beat the dragon."

"One way or another," Sir Pinsky said.

"I'll see you in two days," Rye said. "If I don't make it in time, don't come looking for me. Stay in the castle. I'll find a safe place to wait while the dragon's searching for the sword."

"We'd best get going," Sir Pinsky said. "Goodbye, Rye, and good luck to you."

"Goodbye. Take good care of Barley," Rye said.

"I will," Sir Pinsky promised.

"Goodbye, Rye! Say hello to your selkie friend for me, and tell him thank you!" Barley said.

"I will. See you at the castle!" Rye said.

There didn't seem to be anything else to say, though Rye wished there was. He didn't want to leave Barley, but he knew he had to. With one last wave, Rye turned his horse to the west and kicked him into a gallop.

FOUR

Rye rode through the forest all day and reached the far edge
only as the sun began to set over the Red Mountains. When
Rye came at dusk to the town that Merchant Tropp had told
him to stop for the purpose of changing horses, he felt very
shy about going up to the stable master and presenting him
with the letter. He dismounted from his weary horse and
stood before the stable gate, trying to find the courage to go
in. Then he reminded himself that he'd faced a dragon
yesterday. The stable master couldn't be any worse than the
Dragon of the Deep. Rye unlatched the gate and walked
through.

The stable master read the letter, handed it back to Rye,
and with no questions or any fuss at all, instructed one of his
boys to give Rye the fastest horse they had and send him on
his way. Rye thanked the stable master and on a new, fresh
mount soon left the town behind him.

Rye rode late into the night until he reached another
town, and there he used a few of the coins that Merchant
Tropp had given him to take a room at the inn. He meant to
wake up at dawn as he always did at home, but the sun was
high in the sky when he finally opened his eyes. No time for
breakfast. He jumped out of bed, ran down the stairs, out the
front door, across the street to the stables, and soon was on
the road again.

That noon, Rye rode through the gates of King's Town. He didn't stop until he reached the dock by the river. There at the end of the dock, watching the water, sat the selkie boy in the clothes he'd borrowed from Rye.

Rye dismounted from his horse and called to the selkie.

The boy turned around in surprise. "Oy, I didn't expect you to come from that direction! Got tired of swimming, did you?" The selkie boy walked up the dock until he reached the place where Rye stood on the shore.

"No, that wasn't it. Not really," Rye smiled. It was hard not to feel happy around the selkie boy; he seemed so carefree and friendly. "Here's your skin. Thank you very much for loaning it to me."

"No worse for the wear, I'm sure." The selkie boy took the skin and looked it over carefully. "Seems in good shape. No dragon teeth marks or anything." He winked at Rye. "How did your visit with your brother go?"

Rye told the selkie boy the whole story. The selkie boy's merry grin disappeared when he heard that the dragon would be coming to look for the magic sword.

"You're a brave one now, aren't you?" The selkie boy shook his head. "Now, don't tell me where you hid that sword it in case the dragon comes after me. I wouldn't want to accidentally let it slip."

"Would he do that? Would the dragon come after you?" Rye asked.

"As far as the dragon knows, I am you!" the selkie boy said. "With my skin on, I'll look just like you did when you visited the castle."

Rye hadn't thought of that. "I'm so sorry. I didn't mean to put you in danger too."

"Wait one moment," the selkie boy said. He glanced down at himself, then at the skin. "You wouldn't mind loaning a fellow these clothes a little longer, would you? I've got to get back in the water for a bit right now, but then I could take my skin off and carry it about with me while the dragon's on the prowl."

"You can keep the clothes," Rye said. "They're yours."

"Well then, that's very decent of you. To show you my gratitude, I'll give you a little tip. Listen carefully. The Dragon of the Deep don't answer to nobody or nothing, but he's got a fearsome sense of honor. Get him to swear by his honor, and he'll never break his word. Not ever."

"Thank you," Rye said. "I'll remember that."

"Much obliged to you, my friend." The selkie boy grinned. With the sealskin tucked tight under his arm he ran down to the end of the dock and plunged into the water. A minute later a dark, slick seal's head came up. "Good luck!"

"Thanks," Rye said. "Same to you!"

FIVE

As soon as the selkie had disappeared beneath the water, Rye mounted his horse and rode for the city gate. He had only one day to find Lost Castle before the dragon came looking for the sword. The road ahead of him seemed so long, and after two full days of it he was tired of riding. At the first town he came to he used his letter again to change horses. When he reached the second town around nightfall he wanted to stop and spend the night, but instead he kept going, telling himself that as soon as he reached Lost Forest there would be someone there to guide him to the castle and a nice soft bed. On through the night he rode, alone with the moon in the sky and the stars all around, the road a thin gray ribbon through the velvet dark of the plains. At last the dark ahead grew deeper and a line of trees rose up out of the night. Rye slowed his horse to a walk and entered the shadows beneath the high branches.

The woods lay silent around him. Silent as the dead of winter, though it was only late summer. No insects chirped, no frogs peeped, no owls hooted, no bats fluttered.

"Hello?" Rye called out into the forest.

No answer.

Rye walked his horse along the road until the shadows grew so thick he couldn't see the way anymore. He stopped, tied his horse to a tree, and curled up among the roots to wait for someone or some creature to come and bring him to Lost Castle. Barley had to have found the castle by now, and there would be someone out looking for Rye to fetch him in.

END of Episode Eleven

Episode Twelve: A Dragon's Honor

ONE

Barley and Sir Pinsky had not found Lost Castle at all.

Lost Forest had always been a quiet place, with only an occasional distant birdsong or rustle of a creature moving in the underbrush, but as Barley and Sir Pinsky rode under the trees the only sounds they could hear were the soft plod of their horses' hooves, the squeak of their saddles, and the faint jingle of their bridles. No squirrels, no birds, nothing.

After they'd ridden on for about an hour without seeing a single forest creature, Barley began to worry. "Hello!" he called. "Is anyone here?"

No answer.

Barley shouted most of the day until his voice was hoarse. When night came, he and Sir Pinsky found a clearing and built a crackling fire. No wolves howled. No night creatures scuttled. The forest was empty of life, except for one man and one boy and their two horses.

The next day, Barley tried a different strategy.

"Trees, do you know the way to Lost Castle?" he asked the trees around them.

The trees, as usual, said nothing.

Barley climbed up into the branches of the tallest tree and put his head out above the tops of the leaves. "Good morning, sun!" he called to the sun in the sky. "Can you see where Lost Castle is?"

The sun, perhaps, was too far away to hear him. At any rate it shone down in brilliant silence, distant and stately as it always was.

A light breeze ruffled the leaves and Barley asked, "Wind, do you know the way to Lost Castle?"

The wind changed direction, and Barley became hopeful, but by the time he had slid down the tree branches and dropped to the ground, the wind itself had died completely.

The forest lay absolutely deathly still. It seemed like even the trees had stopped growing.

There was nothing to do but keep searching and hoping.

Barley and Sir Pinsky rode all that second day, beginning at the place where they had camped the night and moving in an ever-widening circle, hunting for the castle, or for any creatures who might show them the way. They knew they had to find the castle by tomorrow afternoon, or the dragon would come for them.

"Don't worry, Barley, if we can't find Lost Castle I will fight and slay the dragon for you." Sir Pinsky tried to sound brave.

"But why would the dragon stay around long enough to fight you?" Barley asked. "All he wants is to take me back to his palace. As soon as he sees the sword, he's free to grab me and go, and then I'll never see Rye or Mother and Father again."

They kept searching, though it seemed more hopeless by the moment.

TWO

That night they didn't sleep but rode all the way until dawn. They tracked back and forth across the forest, though they knew they couldn't look at every inch of it before afternoon. They both grew so weary that it seemed the best thing to do would be to give up.

"I'll keep looking." Sir Pinsky yawned when the morning was half gone. "You can rest here, Barley. There's nothing alive in this blasted woods, so I can't think of what might trouble you while I'm gone."

"No," Barley said. "We mustn't get separated. What if you should be lost?"

"We're both lost already," Sir Pinsky said.

"At least we're lost together," Barley said.

They slid off their horses and slumped to the ground.

Barley stared at the bright bits of sky through the trees, thinking of how marvelous it was to be on the land and how much he was going to miss it. Nearby, the weary horses hung their heads and shuffled their feet. Sir Pinsky started to snore.

The thought that only a few hours from now he'd be back in the clutches of the dragon squeezed at Barley's heart. He sat up and gave one last weary shout. "Hello! Is anyone there? Hello, can someone help us please?"

There came a light crash as if something was bounding through the woods. The sound moved closer and closer. Barley poked Sir Pinsky with his toe, and Sir Pinsky was up with his sword in his hand in a wink.

"Has the dragon come?" Sir Pinsky roared. "I'll deal with that beast! Stand back, Barley!"

"It's too early for the dragon," Barley said. "Something else is coming."

Far off through the trees, Barley caught a glimpse of brown and white.

"It's my deer!" Barley said. "I know it is, the one I rescued when it was a fawn, from the swamp! He's come for us!"

It was true. The deer bounded into the clearing, panting. "Barley," the deer almost sobbed. "I've been looking everywhere for you. You're in terrible danger. The witch says her magic has told her that the Dragon of the Deep is coming to our forest, looking for you! All the other animals have either fled the forest or are gathered at the castle, and you must come too, right away. The castle is the only place that you'll be safe."

Sir Pinsky put the sword back in its sheath.

Barley threw his arms around the deer's neck. "Thank you for coming for us," Barley said.

"Hurry," the deer said. "We have a long way to go."

Knowing that the castle was ahead gave Barley and Sir Pinsky the will to go on. They urged their tired horses as fast as they could go and followed the impatient deer who kept bounding ahead and then dashing back to them. The sun rose higher until it passed the point of noon and still the castle was nowhere in sight.

"Is it close?" Barley asked.

"So long as the witch hasn't moved it," the deer said. "If she's moved it, we're lost for certain."

Lower the sun sank, and lower, and Barley knew that if they didn't reach the castle soon, the dragon would be upon them.

Then at last they saw the towers of the castle through the trees ahead. At the very same moment, Barley heard a terrible roar shake the forest.

The dragon had come.

"Run!" the deer shouted.

The frightened horses galloped toward the castle gate. Barley thought at any instant the dragon would appear behind them, ready to snatch him away. The wolf guard saw them coming and parted to let them through the open gate. Barley checked over his shoulder as his horse galloped into the castle courtyard with Sir Pinsky's horse alongside. Outside the closing gate behind him he thought he saw a streak of sea-green flash through the forest, and his heart stopped. They had reached the castle, true, but if the dragon picked up their tracks, he could still follow them and find them.

And then everything changed. The trees outside were different, everything was quiet. The castle had moved.

The dragon was nowhere in sight.

Barley slid down from his horse and collapsed against the deer with his arms around its neck. Sir Pinsky dismounted then sat down on the ground with his back against the closed gate and sighed with relief. They had made it.

The castle was packed with forest creatures. Birds covered every inch of the roofs and parapets. Rabbits crowded the stairs, foxes peeked out from the kitchen, bears watched from the dungeon door, squirrels ran everywhere, and deer tried not to step on the mice that scurried around under their hooves.

The witch came out into the courtyard, her arms crossed over her chest, an irritated look on her face. "So what's the meaning of this, calling the Dragon of the Deep down upon my forest?"

"Sorry about that," Barley said. "Rye did it to save me from the dragon."

"Why, you look like you're half dragon already yourself!" the witch exclaimed.

Barley hid his webbed hands behind his back. "We've brought you your sword. I think we're done with it for good now."

"Ah, well then, thank you," the witch of Lost Castle peered out the bars of the gate and suddenly all the trees were different yet again. "I'm going to have to keep moving the castle every three minutes until that dragon goes back to his ocean."

"He only has three days to find the sword. After that the game is over," Barley explained.

The witch harrumphed. "Three days! In that case, I hope you have some entertaining stories to tell to keep me awake at nights. Blasted rotten dragon. May ten thousand barnacles stick to his hide."

"Oh, Sir Pinsky!" Barley said. "What about Rye? We have to go back out and get him."

"No." Sir Pinsky caught Barley's arm. "You must stay here where it's safe."

"I can't leave him out there alone," Barley said. "He came for me when the dragon had taken me. I have to go to him. Please let me go. If the sword's in here, the dragon can't take me."

"The rules of the game said nothing about whether or not the dragon can eat you. Stay here, Barley. Rye would want me to keep you safe," Sir Pinsky said.

"But the dragon's out there," Barley wailed. "I don't know what he'll do. He'll be awfully angry when he can't find the sword."

"I say," Sir Pinsky said to the witch. "Can't you move the castle to wherever Rye is? We could pick him up."

"The castle moves where it wants to go," the witch said. "I can't tell it where. I can tell it to move, but the castle decides the location. If I were telling it where to go, it would be too easy to find."

Barley tried a few times to sneak away, but Sir Pinsky had told every animal in the castle to keep an eye out and make sure he stayed. In the end, Barley sat down by a window and watched the forest change every few minutes. "Be safe, Rye. Please be safe," Barley whispered over and over.

THREE

Far off in a different part of the woods, Rye watched the sun.
He knew the dragon would be out searching for the sword
already, and he had no idea if Barley had made it to Lost
Castle or not.

All day, since he'd woken up that morning, he'd been
riding at random through the forest, hoping to see some sign
of Barley or of Lost Castle. He hadn't seen a single bird, a
single squirrel, or any creature at all.

Rye heard a crack like thunder, though the sky was blue
and there were hardly any clouds. A flash like green
lightning streaked by, moving along the ground so fast that
the leaves whirled high in its wake and the branches on the
trees bent after it.

The dragon.

Rye's horse reared up and charged off through the
woods, throwing Rye in a pile of dead leaves at the bottom of
a small hollow.

Terrified, Rye pulled himself to his feet and looked
around for a place to hide.

No fallen logs, no caves, nothing but trees and sparse
undergrowth.

Rye buried himself in the pile of leaves and waited.

He lay still, breathed softly, and listened carefully. Over
and over the thunder of the dragon passed by with a rush of

wind and the groan of the trees, sometimes near and other times far away. Terrible as the sound was, it was a comfort to Rye. The dragon was still looking. It hadn't found Barley yet. That meant Barley must have made it to Lost Castle.

When the sun had almost set, Rye heard the loudest crack yet, and a great rush of wind tore all the leaves away. The dragon stood in front of him, yellow eyes blazing with fury.

"Where is the sword?" the dragon roared.

Rye had been thinking hard about what he would say if this moment came, if the dragon found him and asked him about the sword, and he had a plan. It had something to do with his favorite trick that he'd come up with while he and Barley were taking sword fighting lessons from Soldier Jack, pretending to retreat while looking for the perfect chance to attack. Shaking, he got to his feet. The dragon towered over him with an angry mouth open wide enough to swallow him in one bite.

"Tell me where the sword is now, or I will lay waste to this land. I'll eat up your village, your kingdom. Everything you love or have ever loved will be consumed."

That was hardly playing fair. Not that Rye was going to play fair either.

"No," Rye wailed. He dropped to his knees and clasped his hands. "Please don't. Don't hurt anyone!"

"I will destroy all unless you tell me where the sword is now!"

"Do you promise that if I tell you, you won't hurt anyone?" Rye said.

"Yesssss," the dragon hissed.

"Do you promise?" Rye begged, "that if I tell you where the sword is, you won't hurt any creature or harm anything in all the Emerald Realm? Ever?"

"Of course. Now where is the sword?" the dragon growled.

"Do you swear it on your honor?" Rye whimpered.

"Yes, yes, on my honor. Now tell me, boy. I grow impatient."

Rye stood up straight and looked the dragon in the eye. "The sword is in Lost Castle."

The dragon's eyes bulged with fury. Then he threw back his head let out a roar that shook the forest to its roots. He lunged at Rye, and Rye thought perhaps the dragon was angry enough to break his promise, or perhaps that the Selkie boy hadn't told the truth, and now he was going to be swallowed. The dragon stopped an inch from Rye and glared at him as if he'd like to tear him to shreds, his hot breath choking Rye with the smell of the sea. Then the dragon whirled away with a crash and was gone.

FOUR

For two more days, Rye wandered the forest, hungry and alone, as the constant thunder of the dragon's passing cut through the otherwise silent woods. He drank from the streams, found a few late berries, and sighed over the food in his saddlebags that had vanished along with his runaway horse. Every moment he worried that the dragon might find Lost Castle after all, but as the days passed and the thunder never ceased, Rye felt his heart lighten with hope.

In the middle of the afternoon on the third day, Rye heard one final crack of thunder, and then utter silence fell over the woods.

Maybe a half-hour later, the first birds passed by overhead.

Rye walked in the direction the birds had come from even though he knew there was only a very small chance the birds had come straight from Lost Castle.

More birds flew by, and then even more. Some of them landed in the trees, took a look at Rye, and then flew away again.

Rye didn't have any crumbs to offer them, so even though he tried to ask for their help they didn't stay to listen.

When the sun was near to setting, Rye thought he heard a shout.

"Hello!" Rye shouted back.

Another answering shout came, and then another, one low and one high. Rye couldn't make out any words, but the higher voice sounded like Barley.

"Barley, is that you?" Rye called.

Something came toward him through the trees, crashing as it went. Rye ran toward the sound and soon saw in the distance his brother's sunshine-yellow hair catching the last light of the day.

Barley jumped off his horse and ran to meet Rye. Laughing with joy and relief, the brothers tackled each other in a hug. Then they stood back and stared as if they couldn't believe they were actually seeing each other.

"Did you ever see the dragon?" Barley asked. "I was afraid he might do something terrible to you."

"The selkie boy told me how to trick him," Rye said. "He's bound by his honor now to never trouble anyone in the Emerald Realms again."

"Hooray!" Barley said.

"You're looking... more like yourself," Rye said.

Barley rubbed his cheek where only one or two scales clung to his face. "It started as soon as the dragon had lost the game, see?" He grinned and held up his hands, which no longer had webbing between the fingers. "I'll be back to normal by the time we get home."

Sir Pinsky rode up to where the two brothers stood. He wiped a happy tear from his eye then reached down to shake hands with Rye. Rye noticed that the magic sword was gone, but that Barley and Sir Pinsky each carried a well-loaded pack.

"Well done, Rye. Well done, Barley." Sir Pinsky put his hand on Barley's shoulder. "I've never had such a fine pair of adventuring companions. Now let's camp for the night, and tomorrow we'll set you on the road home."

FIVE

Barley and Rye went with Sir Pinsky to King's Town and rode quietly up to the castle. When the king heard that the dragon had been bound by an oath to never trouble the Emerald Realms again, he declared that a celebration should be held through all the land. There were to be days of feasting and song and dance, but Barley and Rye didn't want any of it. They only wanted to go home. With the King's permission they went to fetch Old Lumpy from the stables and set out the very next morning.

Not many days later, Barley and Rye rode around a bend and saw their very own Humble Village. There was the well, the houses with daubed walls and thatched roofs, the gardens and the apple trees. Fields spread all around, awash in the gentle song of sheep bells and cowbells, the clang of the smith's hammer, and the creaking of the mill wheel.

As they reached the first houses, the goodwives looked up from sweeping their porches or hanging out their washing and called out surprised welcomes. The women shouted to one another until the whole village had come running. There was Soldier Jack, Jep and Tildy, Tom Cobbler, Janet, all of their friends. So many people gathered around that Old Lumpy could hardly move through the crowd.

"Run and tell the Fields their boys are home," someone called out.

"No, wait," Barley said. "We want to tell them ourselves."

The crowd parted and the boys rode to the far side of the village. The sun shone low over the fields, the first bundles of the wheat harvest stood by rows of uncut grain, and in the long shadows lay the hint of autumn coming on. Up ahead the boys saw a little whitewashed cottage with a mossy thatched roof and a string of smoke coming out the chimney. They smelled bread baking and a stew full of sweet vegetables from the garden.

A happy shout rang out that warmed them both right down to their toes. Father Fields had spied them coming. He threw down his rake and leaped over the fence to meet them in the road. Barley jumped down from Old Lumpy's back, right into his arms. Rye climbed down after. Mother came running out of the house, laughing and crying for joy, and all four of them held each other tight for a long, long time before going inside to sit down to supper.

The tale ends well, that's all there is to tell!

END of Season One

Look *for more great adventures*
With Barley and Rye

Discover more great fiction at
www.FictionVortex.com.

Please Leave me a review!
If you enjoyed this book, it really helps if you could take a minute
to leave a review. I promise, I read them all! And keep reading to
find out where you can find more great faerie tales like this one!

Greetings from Fiction Vortex

IF YOU HAVE GOTTEN this far, hopefully you are looking forward to reading more of The Realm Where Faerie Tales Dwell and other Fiction Vortex™ StoryVerses™. You're in luck! We have a whole bunch of episodes available. Head on over to www.FictionVortex.com to get all the latest.

Fiction Vortex is all about episodic fiction like the stuff you just read. We are powered by the collaborative writing software known as StoryShop (a project we have helped birth in order to spread our fiction faster!) Thus far, our StoryVerses™ have been a crazy stupid success, but our baby is still so young and frail!

We are happy to grow strong on the milk of brilliant genre fiction until our bones can withstand the slings and arrows of publishing's lumbering giants. At Fiction Vortex™, we are so brazen to assume we can, nay WILL, pioneer the future of digital storytelling. We scoff at the idea of ebooks being the end all of digital publishing.

Let's work together to restore the intimate bonds and direct collaboration between storyteller and audience. Let's use the technology at our fingertips to do so. Become an integral part in discovering the new balance in written storytelling—a balance forged by reader and writer together.

Additional Faerie Tales Series

We invite you to search the store for any and all of these additional series from within our Realm Where Faerie Tales Dwell StoryVerse™. There are several more great Seasons to devour, and we are continually publishing new Seasons in these series and others. Happy reading!

- ❖ Pieces in the Cinders by Emilee King
- ❖ Rose Red by Jessica Parker
- ❖ The Dragon's Maid by Alison Miller Woods
- ❖ Bean Finds a Pet by Alison Palmer
- ❖ Becoming Cinderella by Lecia Crider

You can sign up for Faerie Tales email updates by going to www.FictionVortex.com.

ABOUT THE AUTHOR

Rebecca J. Carlson lives on the North Shore of Oahu where she can walk from her own front door to a jungle hike in the mountains or a relaxing day at the beach. She teaches college physics, plays the Irish harp, and loves to read and write stories.